UNFIT TC

KJ Charles

Published by KJC Books

Thank you for reading. If you enjoy this book, reviews are very welcome.

Published by KJC Books

Cover by Lexiconic Design

Edited by Veronica Vega

ISBN 978-1-912688-09-8

For Sherene Khaw
with thanks for a great title

Chapter One

It was a bleak, miserable, cold November day when they buried Matthew Lawes. That seemed entirely fitting. He had been a bleak, miserable, cold November of a man.

Gilbert Lawless stood hunched against the penetrating gusts of wind and rain as his half-brother was committed to eternal rest in the family vault. He didn't want to be here. His attendance had been commanded by his uncle Jessamy, and that letter had gone straight on the fire, only to be followed by a second, this one from Jessamy's younger son Percival. Percy was the only member of his family that Gil wouldn't happily have consigned to the eternal flames, so he had read the letter to the end, which meant he'd seen the assurance that he would find it profitable to attend.

He doubted that. Matthew, the much older and only legitimate son, had hated Gil, the living reminder of their father's self-indulgence, and showed it in word and deed; the idea that he might have left Gil anything in his will was a truly twisted joke. But Percy had insisted, and enclosed a ten-shilling note for the railway fare, and after all, Gil had thought, perhaps there might be some answer, some resolution, *something* to be gained here, if only the satisfaction of seeing Matthew go into the ground.

It was not a satisfaction. It was a cold, wet, dismal mulch of misery, and the other people clustered around the vault weren't helping.

Uncle Jessamy looked corpselike himself, his sagging, wrinkled face wrapped in a white muffler that brought winding-sheets irresistibly to mind. His older son Horace had an expression of pinched misery as the rain drove into their skin like needles, but there was satisfaction in his eyes. Matthew had lived as a miserly recluse for the last thirteen years. Jessamy would doubtless inherit a very substantial fortune, and since he probably wouldn't last another year, it would all come to Horace soon enough. Gil just hoped Jessamy would remember to leave Percy a little something, since he wouldn't see a penny after Horace inherited. The Lawes family wasn't known for its brotherly love.

The parson droned out the final platitudes of farewell to Matthew's carcass, and they were free to go at last. Horace walked solicitously beside his doddering father, heading for the carriage with the Lawes arms on the side. They could all have fitted in that, but Percy had explained it wouldn't seem respectful to have just one carriage in attendance. What he'd meant was that Jessamy and Horace wouldn't deign to share a vehicle with a disreputable mulatto bastard. That was fine by Gil; he didn't want to share one with them.

"Great heavens." Percy took off his tall hat, the cheap silk streaked with rain, and gave himself a shake like a dog. "I am chilled to the bone. Do you suppose they might have lit the fires? Maybe the kitchen hearth?"

Gil gave him an appalled look. "You're not serious."

"Matthew kept the place so cold I'm surprised it hasn't rotted away, the old– That is–" Percy stumbled to a stop.

"The tight-fisted miserly old hunks," Gil supplied, not feeling inclined to give respect to the dead that he hadn't to the living.

"Oh, Gil. You're not going to be awkward, are you?"

"I didn't ask to come. What is this about, anyway? Don't tell me Brother Scrooge had a change of heart and left me his fortune."

"No indeed. It, uh... I honestly think you'll have to see."

"See what?"

"Well, what I want to show you," Percy said. "I don't think I can explain. Um, how are you anyway? You look well. Have you been..." He searched for a word. "Comfortable?"

"I've not been arrested, if that's what you're asking."

Percy flushed. "I've a right to worry. I wish you wouldn't."

"I'm sure Matthew wished that too," Gil said. "Bringing down the family name." Or at least the parody of it his father had bestowed upon him, since naturally the bastard son of a Lawes should be dubbed Lawless. He had cared once about being marked out by his surname; later he'd wished to share Matthew's name only so that he could disgrace it. It would have served the swine right.

"I don't give a tinker's curse what Matthew thought, with due respect and all that. I'd just rather you had some other occupation."

"I'll do what the devil I like," Gil said, with the friendliest tone and the laziest smile at his command. Percy's look of concern faltered and faded. Gil felt a pulse of sour satisfaction that almost immediately turned to guilt.

He oughtn't snipe at Percy. None of it was his fault, and he'd gone out of his way for Gil in the past. But he was still a legitimate Lawes, and as such, Gil was damned if he'd listen to any requests, still less any criticism of his occupation. The Lawes had held far too much power over Gil for far too long, in their several poisonous ways; he was damned if he was going to let them affect him any more.

Wealdstone House was indeed warm, with fires blazing in every hearth, and lamps lit against the imminent twilight, since it was three o'clock when they arrived. Evidently Jessamy's old bones and faded eyes required plenty of candles and coals. It had been like that in Pa's time; he had never stinted on making his household comfortable. Matthew was probably turning in his vault.

Gil had spent his childhood here under his father's carelessly affectionate eye. The old man might have played the fool, or the knave, with his housemaid, but he had never failed in his financial obligations to their son, and had formally acknowledged Gil his own when she'd died. That was more than many would have done. Gil had been christened with his mother's surname and inherited her looks; Pa could well have avoided presenting the county with a brown-skinned proof of his misbehaviour. Instead, he'd renamed his bastard to make quite sure there was no doubt, and taken him in, and Gil had lived at Wealdstone House when he wasn't at boarding school until he was sixteen years old. Then his father had died, and Matthew had inherited, and Gil had never seen the place since.

There are standing orders to the servants, Matthew's man of business had said. *If you set foot on the property you are to be whipped.*

Percy was looking at him as he handed his coat and hat to a footman. "How does it feel to be home?"

"This isn't my home."

"It's your home as long as I'm here," Percy said stoutly.

"That is not yours to decide, Percival." That was Horace, emerging from the drawing room with a glass of sherry in his hand. The sombre black of his deep mourning garments did nothing for his cadaverous face. The world being what it was, Gil did not find it a matter of great practical convenience that he'd inherited his looks, complexion, and hair almost entirely from his mother, but infinitely better that than resembling this horse-faced misery. "Wealdstone House is my father's now—I say this with the greatest sorrow for the tragedy that has made it so—and Gilbert is here at his sufferance."

"No, I'm here at his invitation," Gil said. "So why don't you tell me why that is, instead of pretending you aren't delighted Matthew's shuffled off."

"You are a disgrace," Horace said, words dropping cold as stones. "Have you no family feeling?"

"Are you taking the piss?" Gil asked, relishing the way Horace, and Percy too, flinched at the obscenity. "He was a miserly old hunks—Miss Havisham without the wedding dress, or the charm—and I doubt there's a living soul sorry he's dead."

"It doesn't matter," Horace snapped. "I refuse to argue with you, Gilbert. My father commanded your presence—"

"*Invited.*"

"—because, distasteful though it is, you may be able to make yourself of use to this family."

"Not if I can help it."

"Gil." Percy nudged him sharply. "Just listen, would you?"

"Did you tell him?" Horace asked. Percy shook his head. Horace sighed meaningfully. "Well, the fact is that Cousin Matthew– It seems, rather, that Matthew was, that he collected– or I should say, had an interest–that his library–" He made an irritated noise, fished in his pocket, and drew out a key. "Go and show him, Percival."

Gil looked from Horace's discomfort to Percy's pink cheeks. "Show me what?"

Gil stood in what had once been his father's private study, looking around, hands on hips. Once he was absolutely sure of what he was seeing, he drew a long breath. "Well, I'll be blowed."

"Quite," Percy said. "You see the problem."

The room had changed since Gil's day. Not entirely: the old desk was still there, its green leather top more faded, and his father's row of ornate, antique silver snuffboxes on the mantelpiece was in place. Gil had used to play with those as a special treat. Although–

"Where's the seventh snuffbox?"

"What?"

"There used to be seven. The one that looks like a house has gone. Did Matthew do something with it?" The idea was painful. Of course the snuffboxes had become Matthew's on their father's death, along with everything else, but he'd never cared about them, not like Gil had. "He didn't sell it, did he?"

"I have no idea," Percy said. "Is that really the most interesting thing in here?"

It was to Gil, but that was stupid. The snuffboxes had just been a borrowed toy for special occasions, and now they belonged to Jessamy. They didn't matter. He ought to be looking at everything else in here, because there was plenty to look at, starting with the shelves of books.

New books. Not his father's old leatherbound volumes of Fielding and Pierce Egan—those were all gone—but a new and varied collection, some beautifully casebound, others cheap card. Gil knew these books. He'd read many of them. Come to that—

"For God's sake," he said, striding to the bookcase to pull out *Miss Tickler's Tales.* "I *wrote* this one."

Percy winced. "I don't want to know."

The room held perhaps a hundred books, and every one Gil recognised was pornographic. There were the familiar spines of many and varied Holywell Street publications, plenty of the great filth-monger William Dugdale's publications, two more of Gil's own work, and he'd bet *that* would have ruined Matthew's fun if only he'd known. He scanned the shelves, incredulity vying with professional interest. Plenty of flagellation, plenty of tribadic stuff, all the usual ins and outs...and at one end of a high shelf, an elderly volume bound in dark red leather. The spine had no title visible, only the faded remnant of a gilt-stamped monogram that vaguely resembled a crow if you squinted, and brought the hair up on Gil's arms.

Surely not. It couldn't be.

He reached up to pull it out, very carefully, and opened it to the title page. And there it was. *Jonathan: or, The Trials of Virtue.* No author given. Single volume. Private printing, with no details of printer or publisher, just the lithograph of the crow. No edition number, because there had only been one.

"Bloody hell," he said.

Percy came to look. Gil tried not to snatch the book away. "What's that?"

"Nothing. Just a book. Something a bit out of the common way, that's all. I wouldn't worry about it."

Jonathan was one of the most precious rarities in his line, a cross between a pornographic novel and a Gothic romance, featuring an innocent young gentleman and the heroes and villains—all male—who pursued him. Rumour named the author as one of Gil's favourite Gothic novelists; it had supposedly been written to commission for a wealthy lord, and privately printed in a run of just ten copies as gifts for the members of his hellfire club. Gil had been allowed as a great treat to read the first chapter when William Dugdale had got his hands on a copy. He had been looking for it ever since, in part because he wanted to know how the story worked out, in part because the right buyer would pay a fortune for it. God knew what this must have cost Matthew but it would have been well into three figures.

He put the book back with a reluctance so deep it was almost painful, and made himself glance casually around. Matthew's collection had extended beyond books; there were piles of photographs and daguerreotypes and engravings on the desk, and several shelves of what looked like albums. Gil pulled one out and opened it at random to a slightly blurred image: a plump woman, legs wide, with one finger exploring the dark curls at her cunny.

Percy was looking at the ceiling. Gil raised a brow at him. "Not your sort of thing?"

"Not in these quantities. I dare say I like it as much as the next man, but..." Percy indicated the piles and shelves around them. "Well, it's one thing to fancy an iced bun now and then, say, but this is like standing in a great big confectioner's shop. It makes a fellow feel surfeited."

"I hear you, mate. It's a professional hazard." Gil opened another album, and blinked. "Here's some variety for you. Call it a sausage roll."

"What– Oh my God!" Percy recoiled at the picture. It was a clearer image, a young man bent acrobatically over what looked like a clothes horse, photographed from the side. He had his lips wrapped round the prick of the man who stood in front; behind him was a magnificently moustachioed fellow wearing guardsman's boots, an impressive cockstand, and nothing else. He held a whip in meaningful fashion.

"For heaven's sake," Percy said. "Put it away."

Gil skipped a few pages and saw an image he recognised. "Blimey. Look at this."

"I am *not* going to look at that."

"All right, but this is connoisseur's stuff. The complete series sold for something like forty guineas a set."

"What?" Percy yelped. "*How* much?"

"A man could get two years for selling this," Gil pointed out reasonably. "And the fellows in the picture could easily get ten for what they're up to. You've got to charge for the risk."

"I dare say, but forty guineas? That's outrageous!"

"There's some pretty pricey books here too." Gil carefully didn't look at *Jonathan*. "Matthew must have spent hand over fist on this lot. As you might say."

Percy gave a yelp of laughter, then clapped his hand over his mouth like a schoolboy. "Sorry. House of mourning."

"No, it isn't."

"It will be when Horace finds out how much Matthew paid for all this." Percy shook his head. "So, this is why we wanted you."

"I gathered it wasn't for the charm of my company."

"Well, *I'm* glad to see you." Percy slapped him lightly on the arm. "But, er, yes. The thing is, Jessamy and Horace don't want the servants to deal with this, even just carrying it out to burn it. You know how people gossip in the countryside. Word would spread like wildfire, make the family a laughing stock. Horace has kept the room locked, and been carrying the key in his pocket."

"You think nobody knows, with all the packages this must have taken?"

"Yes, but he never left the house," Percy returned. "Everything came on the carrier. And he'd reduced the place to a skeleton staff, he was letting the house rot away around him. Horace says they'll need to hire a dozen people to bring the place back up to scratch. So I don't suppose anyone was paying a great deal of attention to what he was doing, or cared if he didn't want his study swept. In any case, Horace wants the whole thing kept in the family, and the evidence removed from his sight."

"And he's expecting me to sort this out for him, is he? What's in it for me?" Gil made sure he didn't sound too eager. If he could get his hands on some of this stock, even just *Jonathan*...

"If you mean payment, nothing. Horace won't hand over a penny, he's as much a clutchfist as Matthew ever was in his own way. But he is desperate to be rid of it all as quickly and easily as possible, so he asked me to suggest you, er, well, sell it. To cover your costs," Percy explained, with the natural embarrassment of a decent English gentleman negotiating a bulk transaction of pornography.

Gil blinked. "So if I take this lot away for you, I can keep what I make from it? *All* of what I make?"

"Horace thought it would be an economical method of dealing with the matter, since that way it wouldn't cost him anything to have it removed. And of course he wouldn't want to be involved in the sale. But he, we, had no idea..." Percy trailed off, looking around at the heaps of images and shelves of books. "There is quite a lot, isn't there?"

"Just a bit."

"Some of it quite valuable?"

"You might say that."

"Forty guineas for one set of photographs? Just one?"

"They wouldn't all be worth anything like that."

"No, I'm sure. Still. I don't suppose he'd have said you could keep all the proceeds if he'd known it was worth this much."

"I'm sure he wouldn't," Gil agreed, mind racing. The trick would be ensuring he got *Jonathan* in whatever deal he made, without letting Horace know he wanted it–

"On the other hand," Percy went on thoughtfully, "Horace did propose the arrangement himself. And told me very firmly to be of use for once in my life and get it done. And I would hate to disturb him at a time of mourning to discuss money. It would be terribly crass."

"It wouldn't do to be crass," Gil agreed. "Reckon we could avoid that?"

Percy gave him a sharp smile. "Fifty fifty, and we don't trouble Horace with the sordid details."

"Come off it. Seventy thirty. I'm doing the work and taking all the risk."

"Sixty forty?"

"Done," Gil said, mentally adding *not including Jonathan.* "Since it's for the good of the family."

Percy's eyes brimmed with happy malice. "There. I knew you'd be reasonable."

Packing up the product was more of a laugh than Gil had anticipated having in Wealdstone House ever again. Percy worked with him, piling books and photographs and lithographs haphazardly into crates. It took the rest of the day to get it all boxed, and they chatted and laughed the whole time, including while they ate supper together in the kitchen, since Gil wasn't welcome at the dining table that had once been his father's.

He had no desire to mix with decrepit Jessamy or his covetous son anyway. He didn't want the contrast to remind him of this place as it had been, to hear his father's voice down the empty hallways, or mistake the tap of Jessamy's cane for Pa's. And if he had to spend all this time here, packing books and photographs into box after box, it wasn't too bad doing it with Percy. This was the longest they'd spent together in years, since Gil didn't precisely go out of his way to seek out anyone named Lawes. He hadn't seen hide or hair of his relatives after he'd been turfed out of school, and he'd never have spoken to any of them again, except that Percy had gone out of his way to find him.

Not that they were close. Percy held a respectable sort of position in Somerset House, so of course he didn't want to be seen visiting the depraved environs of Holywell Street, and since Gil generally didn't respond to his invitations, they rarely met. But still, he'd made the effort to look Gil up and do him a devil of a good turn once. Gil had asked why he'd bothered, and Percy had said, *You're family.*

Gil took that for what it was worth, which was to say that it and two pennies would get you tuppence worth of tobacco. He knew precisely how much family he had, and what *family* had meant when he'd found himself at sixteen with nowhere to go, no help, no friends, no name. His family had damn near destroyed him once; he wasn't going to give any of them that opportunity again, not even Percy. When it came down to it, you couldn't rely on anyone but yourself, and you forgot that at your peril.

All the same, it was good to have this time together now. Gil told a few stories about his work as they packed, and Percy ended up laughing so hard that the miserable stiff-rump Horace came in, outraged, to remind them this was a house of mourning, and not one Gil belonged in. *Take your filth and get out*, was the message, and that was a lot more what he was used to from the Lawes.

So he did just that the next day, another wet November morning, leaving Wealdstone House for what would doubtless be the final time, with *Jonathan* safely stowed about his person in case of accidents.

The drive from Wealdstone House to the road took an unnecessary loop to give carriages a clear view of the Jacobean building in its magnificence. Gil didn't look back.

The crates were sent up to London by carter, arriving at Gilbert Lawless Bookseller on Holywell Street early on Thursday afternoon. It was a cold, wet day, the air thick with smoke and mist and noisome smells, since the shop was close to Pissing Alley, which served as an escape route onto the Strand in the event of a police raid, and an impromptu privy for less dramatic needs. The wind was blowing from that direction, driving rain onto the cobbles and splashing into the puddles of filth and black mud. It stank like a wet dog out there, and nobody with sense would be shopping for gentlemen's literary entertainment in weather like this, so Gil awarded himself a half holiday, shut up the shop, and settled himself to look at Matthew Lawes' collection. He started with the loose photographs, since they were the easiest carried up the stairs to where he had a fire going.

Gil had been a writer and purveyor of obscene books to the discerning gentleman (and occasionally lady, and a few who stretched the definitions in their own ways) for eleven years now, counting his apprenticeship, and he'd seen a lot. There was very little surprised him any more when it came to what people liked. He didn't make many demands of his own on the occasions he shared a bed, requiring only that his partners should treat things lightly and not expect him to be there the next day; he didn't have the time, the energy, or the spinal flexibility to do a quarter of the things that featured in the books he wrote. But when it came to other people's tastes in copulation, he'd call himself as easy-going as any man in London. It was all just flesh, in the end.

He would not have expected his sour, shrivel-souled half-brother to take that view, but after half an hour he concluded with some astonishment that when it came to fucking, Matthew Lawes had had a mind as open as the sky. There were men with women, men with men, women with women; women dressed as men, men painted as women. Every kind of pairing, and more than pairs because one picture had nine people in a heap. There was speciality stuff too. Plenty of flagellation, carried out with all sorts of implements–whips and canes; leather straps; prickly holly and bunches of furze. There were chains and cuffs; dildos and ticklers; champagne bottles and glasses used for everything but drinking champagne.

It was well outside Gil's professional expertise. He was a bookseller, handling photographs only on the odd occasions they came his way, and he had no idea how to shift this quantity of product without getting nabbed.

He considered the matter. If he took the most valuable sets out, he could probably arrange to sell the rest as a job lot to Arnott on Wych Street. This was an unpalatable prospect, since he didn't much enjoy Arnott's company and indeed considered him highly likely to end up on the front page of the *Illustrated Police News* at some point, but he would prefer to get rid of Matthew's stock as fast as possible even if it meant accepting a bargain price. Percy would doubtless be glad of whatever he got from the sale; Gil just wanted it gone.

Partly he didn't much like having several years' worth of imprisonment with hard labour on the premises, of course. But there was also something about the collection that made him uncomfortable, and he wasn't sure what. It couldn't be the content, which was nothing new. Perhaps it was just the idea of his miserable, stiff-necked prick of a half-brother enjoying himself at all, let alone with such variety. Gil had a buyer, a fellow called Ashbee, who was putting together a collection of every obscene book in the land. Perhaps Matthew too had wanted to own everything possible. Or perhaps it had been a job lot put together by someone else and bought in bulk, and anyway Matthew was dead and gone, so who gave a damn what he'd liked to toss to?

It was irritating to be even thinking about the vicious miserly sod. Gil set back to work, sorting rapidly through photographs, daguerreotypes, and stereoscopic slides in search of dirty gold—and then he stopped.

The image he was holding wasn't particularly noteworthy, just a young man, no more than seventeen, smiling at the camera with his half-full prick hanging out. What caught Gil was that he knew the lad, and he was dead.

Errol, that had been his name. A cheerful cocky sort, always ready with a smart remark, made a fair bit using his mouth in other ways. And he'd been found in Clare Court, a little maze of alleys just a few minutes' walk from Holywell Street, maybe three weeks ago, face battered, skull caved in.

They hadn't found the culprit, and Gil doubted anyone had looked very hard. Errol had spent a fair bit of his short life skittering in and out of cells for indecent behaviour; the police probably thought he'd had it coming. He'd doubtless said the wrong thing to the wrong man at the wrong time, that was all. It happened.

Poor old Errol, though. Gil hesitated over the image, not sure what to do. It seemed disrespectful to sell it on for fist-fucking. Of course Errol wouldn't know, and when he thought about it, how many of the people in these pictures would be dead now? Filthy, foggy London was a maw with iron teeth. People came in their thousands and were consumed. And of course those who sold their bodies were at more risk, girls because they were immoral, boys because they were illegal. They were just product, like the photographs, bought and sold and discarded.

Well, life was hard and there wasn't much to be done about it. Gil stacked up the print with a few more in the series, which showed Errol had made the most of his short term on this earth, and moved.

Chapter Two

"Let me clarify the situation for you, Mr. Aylesford, Mrs. Aylesford."

Vikram didn't consult papers; he didn't need to. The facts of the case were all too familiar. The couple who sat opposite him in Mr. Glaister's office were familiar types too. He was red-faced from years of Indian sun, she had clearly taken care to preserve her complexion with a parasol; neither was used to engaging with an Indian as an equal rather than a subordinate. Vikram was used to that; it was why he dressed with such formal perfection, and let his Oxford education show so clearly in his speech.

He looked from one to the other of the couple. "You engaged 'Flora' as an ayah fifteen years ago, in Calcutta. So beloved and invaluable was she that you had her accompany you back to England, at your request, on the agreement that you would pay her return passage to India. And now that your youngest child is at school and you have no more use for the woman who has cared for your offspring for fifteen years, you propose to abandon her, unwaged, unhelped, on the other side of the world from her home, because it no longer suits you to meet your obligations. A woman who took care of your children all their young lives, who crossed the world because, I quote from your own letter, Mrs Aylesford, you *could not bear to make the journey without our dear Flora*—and what? You will let her eke out a living in a foreign land, if she can, and die in the streets if she can't?"

Mrs Aylesford stared rigidly ahead. Mr. Aylesford was bright red from embarrassment as well as sunburn. Their solicitor looked much as one might expect. Vikram was not making friends.

"There are homes for ayahs," Mr. Aylesford mumbled.

"There is a home for 'Flora'," Vikram said. He couldn't help emphasising the English name, doubtless bestowed on the ayah for the Aylesfords' convenience. She used it herself, after fifteen years. He hated that. "It is in Calcutta, and you will pay her fare according to the offer you made her when you took her from there for your benefit."

"You can't prove we offered that," Mr. Aylesford said. Mr. Glaister winced very slightly.

"No," Vikram said. "I only have her word, and she is only a woman and only a servant and only an Indian. I dare say you thought it would be very easy to cheat her, under the circumstances."

"I resent that remark," Mr. Aylesford said. "I see no reason we should foot the bill for a passage to India when I have a family to provide for. Is a man forever responsible for every servant he may employ? ? She no longer has a position in my household and must make her own way."

"You see no reason to foot the bill. Not honesty? Not British fair play? Not loyalty to a woman who has always been loyal to you? Then try this: I shall represent 'Flora' in court, pro bono, to sue you for her passage." Vikram loved appearing in court; it was his greatest regret about his chosen path in life that he could only do so rarely. "I shall make her case," he went on, slipping into courtroom tones, letting it build. "I shall read extracts from letters written by you; I shall tell the story of how she saved little George, just five years old, from a jackal's jaws; I shall make the jury weep with the tale of her love and faithfulness. And then I shall tell them how you propose to reward it by throwing her on a dust heap, and perhaps I will not be able to take the cost of passage from you, but I *promise* that I will take your reputation. I will have reporters in court, ready to repeat every pathetic detail in tear-wringing fashion. I will make you the most reviled couple in London for your ingratitude." He planted his knuckles on the desk and leaned in, ignoring the tears spilling over Mrs Aylesford's cheeks. "So tell me. Can you afford *that*?"

"That display was hardly necessary, Mr. Pandey," Mr. Glaister said, somewhat stiffly, once the Aylesfords had gone.

"On the contrary. I don't have time to take every one of these miserly swine to court. Have you any idea how many of these women are left, abandoned–"

"I dare say it is very terrible, but your manner to a respectable couple was scarcely what one would expect of–if I may say so–a gentleman."

"I give respect where it's deserved," Vikram said. "Is there anything else? I've work to do."

Faced with public shame for their private greed, the Aylesfords had agreed to pay for a second-class passage to Calcutta.

'Flora' would go home, unlike the dozens of other ayahs abandoned in a foreign land. It was a small victory but he'd take it in the face of what too often felt like a struggle of overwhelming futility.

You can't fight an empire! his father had shouted at him, during one of their many, many arguments, and Vikram had said, *Yes I can. Perhaps I can't beat it, but I can certainly fight.*

It had sounded better then, when he'd been young and fiery and full of belief that India would one day be free of the British yoke. He'd be thirty in a couple of months, and he didn't feel young any more.

Glaister's chambers were in the Inns of Court, not far from his own rooms. He strode back—there was never time to dawdle—let himself in, greeted his clerk, and flopped down at his desk, with its piles of paper neatly squared and stacked for his attention, and the day's post in the middle of the green leather top.

It was the usual mixture. Begging letters. Communications from the various societies he supported—slum improvements, hygiene, universal suffrage, divorce law reform, independence. Requests to speak, requests to give money, requests to give time.

And one scruffy, cheap envelope, addressed only to 'Vikram Pandey' (poorly formed letters but correctly spelled; many solicitors' clerks did not do so well), evidently delivered by hand. Vikram opened it, and pulled out a single sheet of rough paper, inscribed in the same childish writing.

Dear Mr. Pandey

Please will you com my brother is gone away and ma and pa very sad please help us please. He is good boy but gone away.

sincerly

Arabella Gupta

There was an address in Shad Thames. Vikram put the letter down with an internal sigh. He offered legal advice, intervened with the parish and police, and otherwise supported the work of the Shad Thames Eastern Association House, which attempted to provide for Indians who washed up on Britain's shores without the wealth that had smoothed his own path. Lascars, ayahs, visiting students, people attempting to survive as street performers, cooks or carpenters, people who wanted to stay, people who wanted to leave. The displaced, underpaid or homeless souls who gathered there saw him as a beacon of hope, an Indian who was as superior and educated and *English* as any Englishman, and a protector when the law or the parish came knocking. Vikram felt nothing but despair when he walked through its doors.

He was not an enquiry agent, or anything like, to go looking for missing boys, but this might fall within his purview. If the brother had gone for a lascar, working for a fraction of the pay given to white sailors in the hardest, dirtiest jobs on board ship, or had been caught in the meshes of the law, Vikram might be able to help.

He had a meeting in Shad Thames in any case, regarding Association House's lease. So he scooped up the letter, and a few other documents, and set off east.

Some hours later, he was at Miss Gupta's door, a poor, low, dark house on a poor, low, dark street. It would be a crowded home for six, and probably housed at least thirty.

He knocked at the door, and was annoyed to see that action left soot-stains on his knuckles. The white woman who opened it looked at him with a combination of hostility and apprehension. "Who're you?"

"My name is Pandey." He'd been told, often, that he ought to say *I'm not with the police* or *I'm not here to cause trouble*, be a little less towering in his manner and a little less book-learned in his speech. He might as well put on a dirty coat and a cockney accent. "I am looking for the Gupta family. Arabella Gupta. Is she here?"

"Couldn't say," the woman muttered, eyes skittering. "Best come back later."

Vikram glared at her. It had been a long day and there was no sign of it ending soon. "She sent me a letter. I want to speak to the family."

He pulled out the scrap of paper. The woman's eyes moved over it without comprehension. Vikram sighed. "It's from Arabella Gupta. She asked me to visit."

"Asked *you*."

Vikram didn't know if the woman's disbelief and distrust were due to his race or his class and didn't care. The leasehold meeting had been exasperating beyond measure, attended almost entirely by dunderheads who couldn't understand a simple legal document and dullards who wanted only to rehash the question of whether Association House was attracting unwanted sorts to an area that nobody wanted anyway. He wasn't in the vein for any more negotiation. He drew a breath to say so, and almost choked as a piercing squeal came from right behind him.

"Oh, it's you," the woman said. "What's this about inviting gentlemen?"

"Lay off, Meg," said the small child who stood at Vikram's elbow. "Sir, is you Mr. Pandey? Please, sir, come in, thank you. Get out the way, you sour-faced cow! In here please, sir. *Pa!*"

After a few moments of scuffling and shouting in whispers, during which a number of wide-eyed children scurried past,

Vikram found himself in a room that was clearly the Gupta family's home. It was small and dark but no worse than many, with a few sticks of furniture offering a little comfort, and as clean as was possible given the damp and the encroaching black mould on the walls. There were two chairs, one of which was offered to him; the other was occupied by a man either in his fifties or prematurely aged. One of his legs ended at the knee, and Vikram guessed he was or had been a lascar from his weatherbeaten look; he seemed decidedly alarmed. The girl who had escorted him in was, at his ill-informed guess, perhaps eight years old, brown haired, and much lighter skinned than her father.

"Sir, this is my pa, sir," she announced. "And I'm Arabella and thank you for coming, only we don't know what to do because my brother's gone away and Pa says we can't tell the peelers."

Vikram inclined his head to the man, mostly because he had no idea how to speak to a child. "My name is Pandey. I'm a lawyer, I assist at Association House–"

"I know who you are, sir. My name is Anand Gupta, and I beg your pardon but we cannot pay a lawyer."

"I won't charge you anything," Vikram said. As though he'd come to this hovel to seek fees. "Tell me about your son."

"Sunil. He is sixteen, my son from my first marriage. My wife died when he was two years old, and I married Polly ten years ago. We have three children, she and I."

"Six of you. And how do you live?"

"I sell sheep's trotters, on the street. Polly makes trimmings for ladies' hats, artificial flowers and such. Sunil...brought in what he could. He is a good boy."

There was unquestionably an evasion there, masked by the non sequitur. Vikram marked it for later use. "And what has happened to him?"

"I don't know. He did not always come back every night, but now he has not come back at all, or sent to us, for almost three weeks. He always brings money for the rent, the children. Always. He cares for his family."

Vikram pressed a few questions, and got answers that were informative, if not particularly enlightening. Sunil had last been seen on the morning of the twenty-third of October, a Saturday. There had been no word since. He would sometimes spend two or three nights from home but had never been away so long before; he had not told any of his friends where he was going. He had not seemed distressed, or worried, or unusually excited; he had not spoken of plans or fantasies of escape. He had, according to father and daughter, been entirely as usual.

Their fear was obvious, and it was evident that Arabella adored her half-brother. Vikram well knew that was not always the case. "Do Mrs Gupta and Sunil get on well?"

"Very well. He might as well be her son."

Vikram held Mr. Gupta's gaze. "What do you think has happened to Sunil? Do you think he's run away? Gone for a sailor?"

"No," said father and daughter together, and Mr. Gupta went on, "He would not do that. I was a lascar. He means to do better for himself."

"Was there an argument? Any family dispute? A girl, perhaps?" More sincere headshaking. "Then what do you think has happened?" Vikram pressed. "An accident? Have you asked at the hospitals? Have you contacted the police?" And there it was, the giveaway twitch. "Why have you not contacted the police?"

"I told him not to." That was a woman's voice, and Vikram twisted round to see a thin, worn-faced white woman entering the room with a darker infant on her hip. The child gazed at Vikram with huge, solemn eyes. "Bella, you take Joey and get outside. Off, now."

"But Ma!"

"Out."

The girl stood obediently, but as she passed Vikram she clutched at his sleeve with grubby hands. "You will help find Sunil, won't you, sir? You'll find him for us?"

"Out!" Mrs Gupta commanded again, and plonked the infant into the little girl's thin arms, where it looked suddenly huge. The woman shut the door behind her daughter, then walked over and bobbed a curtsey. "You'll be Mr. Pandey, sir. I've first to say, we didn't know Bella was writing to you, not at all. She's a foolish girl with a head full of ideas, and that's the truth."

"She acted with commendable initiative," Vikram said, bristling in instinctive defence. "She is obviously a very bright girl and I trust you will continue her education."

"Initiative is as may be," Mrs Gupta said darkly. "I call it cheek. And as for her education..." She sagged suddenly. "It was Sunil made it so we could put her to school instead of piece work. The last year, he's been bringing in good money and, well, with Gupta's leg, we needed it."

"And how was he making the money?" Vikram asked. "Is this the reason you have not gone to the police?"

"There's no harm in it," Mrs Gupta said, jaw setting. "None in the world. He does errands, for gentlemen."

"Errands for gentlemen," Vikram repeated.

Mrs Gupta's eyes locked with his. Hers were light hazel, lined, tired, and defensive. "He's brought in ten, twenty shillings a week sometimes. He's been taught to speak nice and the gentlemen passed on some good clothes for Gupta, hardly worn. There's no harm in it."

There was certainly no novelty. Boys of the working classes traded their youth for coin as much as girls did. Discussion of that was usually shrouded in the sort of euphemism that Vikram found profoundly irritating in its imprecision, even if it was needful under the law.

It ought not to be. *Prostitution* and *exploitation* were words Vikram thought should be shouted aloud, along with *poverty*. Perhaps the Guptas knew exactly what Sunil did for his money; perhaps they merely suspected, or chose not to question. A growing family with a crippled father could not be expected to turn away the wages of sin when it paid at these rates, no matter what comfortably-off moralists would say. "Did Sunil dislike his way of living?"

"No, sir. He was always cheerful," Mrs Gupta insisted. "He liked having money in his pocket, he was saving a little. He wanted—he *wants*—" Her face crumpled suddenly. Mr. Gupta put up his hand to hers, and she clutched it, work-worn fingers twining together. Her other hand was knotted in the grimy cloth of her apron. "I just want him to be safe."

"Are you afraid for his life?" Vikram asked.

"We don't know," Mr. Gupta said. "We don't *know*."

But they feared to go to the police, as well they might. A foreign boy of the lowest class with such a tale was unlikely to be anyone's priority and might even be arrested if he were still alive. A vindictive policeman might accuse his parents of living off immoral earnings. "Do you know his employer's name?"

The Guptas both shook their heads. "He never said," Mrs Gupta added. "I don't know where he went."

Well, what the devil would you have me do, then? Vikram bit back the angry words. They sprang from the tight knot in his stomach that he always felt when there was help he couldn't give, a problem he couldn't solve. There were so many of them. He understood why people went through life averting their eyes from everyone else's suffering; when one noticed, it was unbearable.

"Please, sir," Mrs Gupta said. "He's Gupta's eldest and Arabella loves him so and—please. Even if the news isn't good. We have to know."

Just say "I can't help you." Just say it. Don't offer false promises.

He couldn't make himself do it. Not this boy, this age. He'd lost one such himself, once. And if Sunil was lying dead somewhere in this sprawling city, if he had already been buried in a pauper's grave for want of someone to claim him, Vikram might at least be able to find that out. He could spare a couple of shillings, send out someone to ask questions.

He pushed a hand through his hair. "I will send around to hospitals and mortuaries." They both flinched. "Is there anything else you can tell me, any clue as to his employer or place of work? And I will need a full description."

The pair exchanged glances. Mr. Gupta nodded. Mrs Gupta went to the corner and lifted the lid of a cheap, battered box. She came over and gave Vikram a framed photograph.

He blinked. Photography was not cheap, and this was a good, clear image in a well-made frame, far better than he'd expect this painfully poor family to own. It showed a handsome, smiling youth with a slight resemblance to Mr. Gupta, an incipient moustache that brought back Vikram's memories of his own adolescence, and a cocky look. A happy, confident young man. "This is Sunil?"

"He gave it to us the Sunday before he vanished," Mr. Gupta said. "He was working as an photographer's model. It was a gift."

Vikram turned over the picture. There was no indication of the studio or the photographer's name. That in itself was suggestive of a photographer who didn't want to be found, and if Sunil had been a 'model' for one of those...

It was, perhaps, a start.

Chapter Three

The next afternoon saw Vikram standing in Holywell Street. He'd never been there before but he knew of it: a sordid little street that ran parallel to the Strand between St. Mary le Strand and St. Clement Danes. People called it the Backside of St. Clement's, and from all he'd heard, it lived up to the promise of that nickname. This was where one came to buy pornographic and obscene works, a thing Vikram had never done in his life.

He had no idea if he could pick up Sunil's trail simply by asking around, based on a perfectly innocent photograph. It seemed unlikely in the extreme, but he had to do something with the memory of Arabella's tug on his sleeve and hopeful eyes on his face. He was fairly sure he could intimidate dealers in illicit wares into giving him some sort of answer. Not that they'd have anything useful to tell him if Sunil had fallen into the Thames or under the wheels of a cab, but it was something to do, so he would do it.

That had brought him along the Strand to here. The Strand was a wide thoroughfare with imposing tall frontages, fit for the capital of empire; Holywell Street was its disreputable, drink-sodden uncle with his trouser buttons undone. It was narrow and lined with sagging Jacobean or even Elizabethan houses, their black timbers barely showing against soot-darkened plaster, with pointed gables and overhanging storeys that conspired together to block out what little daylight there was. The cobbles underfoot were slimy, crusty, and slippery with deposits of soot and mud, worse filth too. There was a pervading scent of urine. A couple of shop-soiled women in dresses that had once been bright lounged against a wall looking at him with an unconvincing show of interest.

It wasn't poor, though. Vikram knew the East End and the docks; he knew the places where people slept twenty to a room in houses rotting away over cesspools that nobody ever paid to empty. He knew what poverty looked like, and it wasn't shops with plentiful goods in the windows, steps free of hollow-faced children and dead-eyed women. Holywell Street's decay was deliberate, if he was any judge. It would rather wallow freely in its filth than bow to other people's ideas of cleanliness.

Twenty years ago, the street would have proclaimed its illegal wares without shame. These days, since the law had put down its heavy foot, the shops just looked shabby and unremarkable. Vikram decided he would start at one end and work his way up and down until he had an answer, or at least somewhere else to look, for the sake of a boy lost in the city and a little sister who missed him.

That was the plan. Within fifteen minutes, it started feeling more like an embarrassment.

Vikram had tried three shops by then. The first proprietor had barely looked at the image before denying all knowledge of Sunil, obscene publications, or the existence of the photographic art. Evidently he'd smelled trouble. Vikram opened negotiations in the second shop by asking about purchase of illicit photographs, but unfortunately, he'd never had a talent for acting. The shopkeeper had denied everything, and threatened to "summons a pleeceman". Vikram took that threat for what it was worth, since he was quite sure the fellow wouldn't want the law in here, but there was no point insisting in the teeth of such obduracy.

He decided to attempt a more conciliatory approach in the third shop. Unfortunately, he was not feeling conciliatory. Also unfortunately, though predictably, as he came in an urchin came scurrying out past him, shooting up a defiant glance, and the shopkeeper was already waiting with his arms folded.

Of course the people of Holywell Street were more interested in their own skins than the fate of a lost youth. It was only to be expected they would lie and deny and band together to fend off enquiry. It still rankled, and Vikram's intention to appeal to the man's humanity and better nature was rapidly forgotten when the shopkeeper told him to piss off for a nark. Vikram shared his opinion of pigs rolling in the sewer of human degradation, and stalked out of the shop in a raging temper.

This was a waste of time. What he ought to do was hire an investigator, someone used to asking questions. Or let the matter go, curse it. What was one more vanished youth in the great abyss of London? Would it not make more sense for Vikram to do the work he knew, and help the people he could?

But that meant giving up, and Vikram hated giving up. More, it meant accepting defeat of a kind that tasted like poison.

It was absurd. There were so many children lost in London all the time, and many of them lost in plain sight, condemned to misery from birth without the love and caring Sunil had obviously known. This one boy wasn't special, except in the way that any human being was special. It was simply that Vikram felt the Guptas' gaping, frightening loss, because he knew it.

That was the problem. He knew how it felt when someone didn't come back, when you demanded why and never had an answer, when you looked around to share a joke or a smile and remembered he wasn't there, when you were still doing it years later because there had been no letter, no funeral, no *reason.* Vikram had looked at Sunil's picture, just sixteen, and seen his own loss, and it had hurt so much all over again.

He stood there in this disgusting street of disgusting men, under drizzle hardening into rain, staring at the filth-encrusted cobbles under his feet for a moment. Then he took a deep breath and set his shoulders. He would not give up the search for Sunil; he would find someone who would give him some sort of answer, or place to look. He *would,* in the name of all the lost people, and in memory of Gil.

Vikram squinted up under his hat-brim at the next shop-sign, and almost fell over.

Gilbert Lawless Bookseller

The sign hung there, once red and gold, now dusted by soot and streaked by rain, but the words were quite legible.

Gilbert Lawless. Gil.

It couldn't be, Vikram thought, with an odd roaring in his ears. There must be dozens of other boys—men, now—with that name. Of course there were; it was only the reawakened memories that were making him imagine otherwise. This could not be *his* Gil Lawless, because his Gil Lawless was missing, vanished, almost certainly dead. This couldn't possibly be Gil, alive and well and...running an obscene bookshop in London's most ill-reputed street...

The appalling plausibility of that dawned on him along with the awareness that if this was truly, really Gil Lawless alive, Vikram was going to kill him.

He shoved open the door. The interior of the shop was very small and cluttered, with the counter in the middle of the room, and behind it a door to a back room and a flight of wooden steps leading up. The walls were lined with books, cheap card-bound editions available to browsers, leather-bound sets of evident quality behind the counter. The gas was lit against the encroachment of dusk, and the chilly air felt at once dusty and damp.

Gil was leaning on the counter.

He'd changed. That was Vikram's first thought; on its heels came the awareness that he would have known him, even without the name on the shop front. He'd have known him anywhere.

Gil at sixteen had already been filling out into manhood, and Gil at almost thirty was not dramatically bigger. He hadn't grown particularly tall, so that Vikram had the advantage of him by a good four inches, and he was of no more than medium build, sinew rather than muscle. His face was longer and leaner, interestingly high-cheekboned now he'd lost his boyish roundness; he had a day's black scruff on his chin. His hair had been kept cropped almost to the scalp at school; it now grew up and out in tight curls for an inch or so. His coat was shrugged on as his clothes had always been, his cuffs and elbows dusty. In fact, he looked exactly as Vikram would have imagined him, if he'd ever imagined the swine was still alive.

Gil was wearing a purely professional smile, which faded as he saw Vikram staring at him. His brows drew together, warily. "Yes, sir? Can I help you?"

They hadn't seen one another since Gil had disappeared from school part-way through summer term thirteen years ago. Vikram had been bewildered, then afraid, then more alone than he'd ever imagined possible. And there had been nothing more, ever: no letter to the school or Vikram's home, no response to the pleas Vikram had sent to Wealdstone House, no result from the search he'd paid for when he'd come down from Oxford. Not one single indication that he *wasn't* dead. Vikram had made himself accept that his childhood friend, the person he'd been closest to in his whole life, was gone and he would never even have a chance to say goodbye. And all the time Gil had been in London, running a shop a stone's throw from Lincoln's Inn, as though Vikram hadn't spent the last thirteen years alone.

It was typical. It was absolutely typical Gil Lawless, the idle, flippant swine. Of course he wouldn't have considered something as trivial as his best friend's terror for him. He'd doubtless moved on and forgotten, shrugging the past off as he'd always shrugged off the insults and abuses Vikram couldn't ignore, and he didn't even know who Vikram was now.

Bloody, bloody, *bloody* Gil.

"Nothing," Vikram heard himself say, and turned away. He would just leave, walk out, abandon this ill-fated quest–

"Hold on," Gil said sharply. "Hoi! Stay there!" A scuff of feet and a thump, as if he'd vaulted the counter, and then Gil's fingers were closing around Vikram's forearm, tugging him round. "Vikram? Vikram. You *are.*"

There was astonishment on his face which gave way for a second to something almost like alarm, and then his face split in a smile of delight that made Vikram think he must have imagined that fleeting look. "Vik. Bugger me."

"Gil," Vikram said, and couldn't find anything else.

"But–" Gil opened his hands. "Vik. I don't know what to say. What are you doing here?"

"You're surprised?" Vikram said. "*You're* surprised? I thought you were dead!"

Gil's mouth opened slightly, then broke into the grin Vikram had never forgotten. "What, me? Wouldn't be seen dead in a coffin."

That was it? That was the sum total of his apology for the way he'd vanished and left Vikram alone and bereft in that miserable hellhole of a school? Vikram found himself speechless, and as he searched for words to convey his outrage, Gil grabbed his hand.

"It's damned good to see you. It really is." His grip was warm and tight. It was a man's hand, calloused at the bases of the fingers, large and strong-boned, but Vikram still felt that old, absurd reaction. As though Gil was going to tug him along to some adventure, some secret, some escape that he'd never find alone.

Gil was right here, alive, and as much as Vikram wanted to wring his neck, he couldn't hold back a smile.

"You're alive," he said, pointlessly obvious.

"Never better. What are you up to? Do you have time for tea? Let me lock the front and come upstairs. I've a fire, and there's no trade to speak of on a miserable day like this. Come on."

He lifted the counter hatch and pushed Vikram through it, towards the stairs, just as though he were still the larger of the two of them, and Vikram found himself no more able to resist than he ever had been. Gil went to the door, bolted it, and turned the sign to show he was closed, then came past and led the way upstairs. Vikram followed him into a small room, which appeared to be at once living space and storehouse, piled as it was with books, bound and unbound, papers, piles of loose photographs, bundles of manuscript, and boxes. There was a blazing fire, which was welcome, and by it a pair of faded but comfortable-looking upholstered chairs, one covered in papers and topped with a black fur stole.

Gil slid a hand under the fur and tossed it up and sideways. It sprouted legs and a very bushy tail, hit the floor lightly, and stalked resentfully away. Gil ignored the cat's annoyance, turfing the papers onto the floor with a casual disregard for their order that made Vikram's teeth hurt.

"Here you go. I don't often have people up here." That was, it seemed, Gil's entire apology for the chaos. "Tea?" He put the kettle on the fire without further consultation, as Vikram hung up his coat and hat on the stand in the corner, and took the chair.

"Well." Gil sat back in his own chair, crossing his legs. "So. How've you been?"

Vikram steepled his fingertips to prevent himself clenching his fists. "How have I been? You mean, in the thirteen years since you vanished out of my life as though you'd never existed?"

"Well. Yes."

"What do you mean, yes?" Vikram demanded. "I came back from double Latin and you were gone! Your clothes were gone, your chest, nobody would tell me anything, nobody answered my letters, you never got in touch *once*, and I didn't have a word from you from that day to this! What the devil happened?"

There was a silence, long enough for Vikram to feel his anger undermined by a current of doubt as to whether he'd sounded quite as calm and unemotional as he'd have liked, then Gil let out a breathy whistle. "Right. You're not taking life any more lightly, I see."

"No, I am not!" Vikram shouted. "Of course I'm not! What do you expect me to–to–"

Quite suddenly, he felt dizzy and airless, as though this were a dream and he'd just become aware of the implausibility of it all. His face was cold and clammy, his hands tremulous. He decided that he could not possibly do anything so weak as to put his head between his knees, and then realised that the alternative might be passing out.

"Jesus," Gil said. "Are you all right?"

"Very well," Vikram said, muffled. "Just give me a moment."

A light hand touched his shoulder. "Breathe, mate. Take your time. Here, I'll make the tea."

Vikram breathed, attempting to force the blood back to his brain by sheer willpower. He sat up after a few moments to see Gil sitting opposite, holding out a chipped, steaming mug.

"I put sugar in it. Feeling better?"

Vikram sipped the brew and grimaced. "I'm perfectly well. I was just taken dizzy, that's all."

"Yeah, I saw. So you didn't come here looking for me?"

"Of course I didn't. I thought you were dead."

"I can see why it came as a shock to say good afternoon." Gil made a face. "Sorry about that."

Sorry. Vikram shook his head and concentrated on the syrupy tea. Gil must have put half the sugar bowl into it.

"You look like you're doing well," Gil said after a moment. "Very smart. What is it, the law? Barrister?"

"Solicitor. I didn't choose to take silk."

"As long as it suits. What else? Married?"

"No."

"How are the old folk?"

"At the same address," Vikram said. "If you were interested in their well-being, a letter would have found them, or me."

"Right. Any use to say I was busy?"

"For thirteen years?"

Gil's face stilled. It wouldn't have stood out to most people, but Vikram had known him better than anyone once upon a time, and he recognised a man taking a second to gather himself when he saw one.

It was only a second, then Gil smiled again, this time somewhat sardonically. "About two minutes before you walked in I had a boy come from number ten to warn me there was some swell wandering around, asking awkward questions about goods that could get a fellow a spell in chokey. I assume that was you, Mr. Solicitor?"

Vikram swallowed a mouthful of tea. "Yes."

"Yes. This is my shop. My name on the sign, right here in the middle of Holywell Street." Gil's smile had entirely faded now. "Do you want to think again about whether you'd have liked me writing to your mother?"

"You didn't always do this," Vikram said. "You didn't *have* to do this."

"Oh, I did. I really did."

"What–" Vikram wasn't sure he wanted to ask. He didn't want to think of Gil in this grimy, illicit business. "What do you do?"

"What happens if I tell you? Do I get the peelers round? Society for the Suppression of Vice?"

"Oh, come on. That's not fair."

"Let's not be sentimental. You went your way and I went mine, and you wouldn't have thanked me for turning up at your door any time in the last few years, so don't give me a hard time that I kept my troubles to myself, all right?"

"No!" Vikram said furiously. "It is not all right. Whatever you've been doing, you were sixteen, and you vanished, and I was *afraid,* damn you. I don't know what you did to be expelled–"

"But you think I did something." Gil leaned back. "Right."

"I wasn't even allowed to ask! I was put in detention for demanding answers. That was what they did when fellows were sacked for stealing, or–unmentionable things." The old slang tasted oddly on his tongue.

Gil smiled tightly. "Of course they did. Hang a dog and then give him a bad name."

"Isn't it the other way around?"

"Hardly matters now. What are you doing asking awkward questions in Holywell Street?"

He'd clean forgotten. Vikram drained the tea, looked around for any reasonable surface on which to place the mug, and gave up, putting it carefully on the floor. As he sat back, the cat took the opportunity to leap into his lap, anchoring itself with claws. He yelped.

"Satan, you arse," Gil said. "Shove him off."

"Your cat is called Satan?"

"He's not *my* cat. He just lives here."

Vikram pushed cautiously and ineffectually at the mass of fur. The cat gave him a malevolent look, kneaded his thigh in a threatening manner, and wrapped itself up to sleep as though Vikram had nothing else to do but supply a lap. "Oh, for– Do something with it, will you?"

Gil grinned. "Don't look at me. Not my responsibility, are you, Satan?"

"That is an appalling name for a cat."

"Accurate, though. You were going to tell me what you're up to."

"As you said, asking awkward questions." Vikram took a deep breath. "I'm trying to find a boy."

Gil's brows slanted. "Any particular boy?"

Vikram tried to stand. The cat, without opening its eyes, extended its claws in a way that suggested it would not be removed without violence. "Damn this creature. Will you pass me my briefcase?"

Gil handed it over. Vikram extracted the framed photograph but held it facing him. "This is a little difficult. I should explain, I offer legal advice to Indians and others at the Shad Thames Eastern Association House."

"You lawyer in Shad Thames?" Gil said. "You're looking better than I'd think on that."

"My office is in Lincoln's Inn. I work pro bono in Shad Thames. It's a damned disgrace, the way poor Indian workers are treated. Paid a pittance and discarded without compunction." Gil wore the very familiar expression of a man who didn't see that this was his concern. Vikram pushed the irritation down. "The result is that I have all sorts of problems brought to my door."

"And what sort of problem brings you to Holywell Street?"

Vikram needed help; Gil was in a position to help him, appalling though that was to consider. The question was whether his obviously flexible morality was sufficiently flexible for this. Vikram had seen too many criminals outraged over other people's transgressions to take that on trust.

But he couldn't really believe Gil would play the righteous man, and in truth he had little choice.

"A boy aged sixteen has vanished," he said. "It seems that he was keeping company with older men."

"Ah."

"He disappeared three weeks ago. Perhaps just an accident, but..."

"Got you."

"And he had had this picture taken," Vikram said. "Obviously expensive, no studio name, and his parents told me that he had been working as a photographer's model."

"I see why you came to Holywell Street."

"Nobody else did," Vikram muttered.

Gil snorted. "Nobody's going to start telling the truth to a passing swell. Are you trying to find the photographer or the gentleman friends?"

"Either, or both. Whatever I can."

"And why are you doing this?"

"His parents have no means to find him, and they can't go to the police under the circumstances."

"No, but what I mean is, why do you care what happens to some lad gone mollying?"

Vikram shook his head. It was almost funny. Almost. "If you understood what it is to have someone for whom you care disappear, if you had *any idea* how it feels not to know, you would not ask me that."

Gil's smile died on his lips. His eyes were on Vikram, intent, and there was something at once achingly familiar and very different in their look. All of him was familiar and different, and it occurred to Vikram, irrelevantly but forcibly, that his old friend had grown up a very handsome man.

"Vik," Gil said. "Mate..."

He leaned forward. Without conscious volition, Vikram did the same. The cat's weight shifted with his movement, and a set of claws dug savagely into his thigh. "Ow! Damn it!"

"Chuck him off," Gil recommended, sitting back. "Ah, hell. All right, let's see your picture."

Vikram held out the photograph as best he could without incurring further attack. "Here. His name's Sunil Gupta."

"Indian. Right," Gil said, frowning at it. "That should...help... I've seen him. I swear I've seen him."

"You *know* him?"

"Know? No. Look, Vik, joking aside, you understand what I sell here?"

Vikram wanted to say yes, of course he did. Gil had always been the worldly one, initiating his naive friend into the mysteries of life. Vikram had no desire to resume that relationship. He was an experienced professional man, and his work had left him well acquainted with sordor, crime, and degradation.

But, undeniably, this was a form of sordor, crime, and degradation that up till now, he had managed to avoid.

"Not entirely," he said. "That is, I'm well aware of this street's reputation but not familiar with the, uh, goods themselves."

"Goods." Gil grinned briefly. "Yes, well. What you get round here, under the counter as it were, is literature tending to deprave or corrupt. Obscene publications. Books mostly, but also photographs. Anything that's unfit to print."

"Why?" Vikram demanded. "You had brains, you were better than this." He saw Gil's face close over, but he couldn't or didn't stop himself. He dealt with exploitation every day in its many and varied forms—men exploiting women, white exploiting brown and black, rich exploiting poor, anyone above treading on whoever was below. The sale of poor bodies for the entertainment of the rich was enraging; the idea of Gil involved in it was sickening. He needed it not to be true. "Why would you take up this filthy business?"

"Money," Gil said. "And why not? People must be amused, like the man said, and this is how they like to amuse themselves. The law says people shouldn't fuck and mustn't fuck and oughtn't think about fucking. Well, you tell *them* that. If they didn't want it, they wouldn't come and buy it."

"People want a number of things that aren't good for them."

"That's their problem."

Gil's voice was flat. Vikram reminded himself that he needed help. "We will have to disagree, but in any case, I interrupted you. Go on."

"Well. Some of the things people want, the law doesn't allow 'em to have, or do. So if you're going to take a high moral tone, or call the Society for Suppression of Vice down on me as an act of Christian charity–"

"I'm not a Christian."

"Figure of speech."

"No, it isn't. I am not a Christian," Vikram repeated. "Had you forgotten that?"

"You aren't, are you. And that makes a difference, being Hindu?"

"By being an entirely different philosophy?" Vikram suggested, not restraining the sarcasm. "My religion holds that mutual affection and pleasure are a good thing, an aim of human life."

"You want to get some missionaries out round here, mate. I can see that catching on."

"I don't mean at the expense of decency. And this is a digression. I intended only to say that I am not nearly so concerned by the...the acts committed, as the fact that people are forced to them. I do not care whether Sunil sold himself to a man or a woman; I care that he had to sell himself at all, and that he may have died for it. *That* is what I am here for, and nothing more, and you know very well I will not report you to the authorities for anything you tell me."

"Do I?"

Vikram's breath caught in his throat with outrage and hurt. He inhaled sharply in order to embark on a furious response, but the rueful look on Gil's face stopped him before he started. "Yes, I do. Sorry, Vik. That was uncalled for."

"Yes, it was," Vikram snapped. "But if you want my word of honour, you have it."

Gil nodded acknowledgement, his lips already curving into a smile again. "Good to know. Though you can't blame a man for thinking you aren't a natural lawbreaker. All right, let me see if I can find this picture, and I'm not making promises it's the same boy. I could be wrong." He hauled himself out of the chair, went to the desk, and picked up a small sheaf of photographs through which he began to sort. Vikram looked into the fire, waiting, unsettled. After a few moments, he became aware that he was stroking the cat. It would doubtless leave hair all over his trouser legs. He didn't even like cats.

Gil returned to the fireside, holding out a photograph. "Here it is. Don't say I didn't warn you."

Vikram looked at the image, and couldn't hold back the flinch.

It showed a young Indian man, naked but for socks and suspenders. He was adolescent, with a swagger in his stance despite his exposure, and he looked very like the framed picture of Sunil.

"Yes. I think this is him. And again there's no studio mark on the back. Would you say the photograph looks recent?"

Gil leaned on the edge of Vikram's chair. He smelled of paper and ink and dust, the scent of books, with a lower note of...not quite musk. Maleness. "Well, the print's in good condition. And he looks about the same in both, and boys change fairly quick at his age. How old's your picture?"

"He gave it to his parents a month ago."

"Right." Gil chewed his lip. "So here's your lad who's had a gentleman friend, or several, for a while?"

"At least a year."

"But also—or instead of?—he's doing *poses plastiques,* quite recently."

"Maybe he fell out with his gentleman friend, and he needed a new way to bring the money in," Vikram suggested. "Maybe he posed for the photographs and the gentleman wasn't happy when he found out."

Gil shrugged. "Maybe the gentleman was the one who arranged the pictures and was pleased as Punch to see them."

"Is that likely?"

"Why not? There's plenty of people who like looking at pictures."

"Do you know who takes these things?"

"Any fool with a camera. Well, and a dark-room and some willing lads or ladies, but those aren't hard to come by."

Vikram nodded. "Where did you get this one?"

"Believe it or not, my half-brother."

"Your— *Matthew*?"

Vikram had never met Matthew Lawes. He'd never met Gil's father either, or been to Wealdstone House, since the old man's acknowledgement of his bastard hadn't extended to having his friends come to visit.

"Oh, yes," Gil said. "Turns out he had a taste for literature tending to deprave or corrupt. Apparently it runs in the family. Most of what's in here was his, the books and such."

Vikram looked around at the heaps. "Are you serious?"

"No joke. The family asked me to get rid of it after he died. I was going through it to price it up when I noticed Sunil."

"That's something of a coincidence."

"Well, you don't see that many people of our colour, that's why I remembered. I could have flicked past any number of missing white boys. There's at least one murdered lad in there."

"I beg your pardon?"

"A boy I knew. He was killed a few weeks ago, on the street, skull stoved in. It's a dangerous game, and people get hurt. The police won't help, and you're mostly on your own." Gil grinned briefly. "Last time I saw him, Errol was talking about setting up a trade union, to stop the workers being ripped off."

"Good for him," Vikram said absently. "When was this unfortunate killed?"

Gil frowned, counting on his fingers. "I heard on a Monday morning with the delivery so... The twenty-third, Saturday evening. He was killed that night, and found the next morning. Why?"

Between the fire and the cat on his lap, Vikram was almost uncomfortably warm, but he nevertheless felt a cold sensation along his spine. "Sunil left his home for the last time on the morning of the twenty-third."

They looked at one another.

"How big a world is this?" Vikram asked. "Would one young man who posed for these pictures have been likely to know another?"

"Maybe." Gil rapped his knuckles against the side of the chair. "Might've."

"I wonder if I now take this to the police."

Gil made a face. "Eh. It's not the safest profession. You *expect* unnatural deaths in this line now and again."

"Which line? The photographs?"

"Renting. Which is to say, boys with gentlemen friends. Errol had plenty of them."

"How do you know?" Vikram asked, then felt his cheeks flame. "I mean... No, damn it, *how* do you know?" He heard the harshness in his own voice and, quite clearly, so did Gil.

"How'd you think?" Gil moved away from the chair with a twist of his body that drew Vikram's attention unavoidably to his lean hips, and folded his arms. "I sell filth, mate, and a fair bit of it's for men who like men. I know what's what."

Vikram had no idea how to respond to that. He didn't even know why he'd asked. He *shouldn't* have asked, because now there were a dozen other things he wanted to ask, all worse. A pulse ticced in his jaw, a distracting throb of sensation.

Gil went on. "Both boys were in the same line of work, and it's not a safe one. That seems to me the only connection that counts. Yes, my half-brother had photographs of them both, but he had a lot of photographs."

"When did Matthew die?"

"The first of November." Gil's brows slanted comically. "I like your thinking, but it's no go. He had a stroke on the twenty-first, never regained consciousness."

His tone didn't suggest condolences would be welcome. "Right. Nevertheless, for one boy to die and one disappear on the same date—"

"Maybe. But if you go to the police with nothing more than this, all that'll happen is they'll do me for obscene publications, and pick up a lot of other fellows who never did any harm."

"This is harm," Vikram said, dropping the photograph on the arm of the chair. The cat stirred on his lap. "This is not what young men—or women either—should be doing."

"You give 'em another way to keep their bellies full and clothes on their backs and I'm sure they'll take it."

That was true enough. Vikram took a steadying breath. "I wonder whether your half-brother's collection has any more secrets. I understand that he had a lot of pictures, but even so. Did he keep them in any order?"

"They're mostly in albums." Gil jerked a thumb. "I haven't looked at those yet. There are a lot of loose ones too, but if they were in order before, they aren't now. I didn't pay attention when I packed the boxes up."

"Mph." Vikram tapped his fingers against his lips, thinking, and saw a grin dawn on Gil's face. "What is it?"

"You always did that." Gil imitated the gesture—forefingers steepled together, other fingers interlaced, tapping them against his own lips. "Whenever you were coming up with something."

"I wish I were." Vikram disengaged his fingers with some self-consciousness. "Have you looked through all his pictures?"

"Not yet. I only got them yesterday."

"Perhaps you should start there."

"Start what?"

"Well, looking of course," Vikram said, a little impatiently. "For this Errol, and Sunil. For anything that might identify the photographer." He was tapping his lips again, dammit. He lowered his hands hastily. "We'll need to go through that in detail, and also to ask about other missing young men. Can you enquire within your, uh, circle of acquaintance, and see—"

"Whoa there," Gil said. "This isn't my problem."

It was like a splash of cold water to the face. "What do you mean?"

"I've got a business to take care of, and not one that'll be improved if I go around pretending to be a peeler."

"But there's a boy dead. Another missing. Someone has to look into this, and I don't have the faintest idea how to find out about–" He gestured at the piles around them.

"Good. You don't want to start snouting around in this business."

"What else am I to do?" Vikram demanded hotly. "I can't go to the police!"

"Nor can I," Gil snapped. "Not to ask about a renter, and not to talk about the roomful of illegal pictures I 'inherited from my brother'." He pantomimed a policeman's incredulity as he spoke. "I need to get this lot off my hands, and that's all I want to do."

"And what about Sunil?"

"What about him?"

Vikram drew in an angry breath, and saw Gil's expression flicker, just slightly. "Are you serious?"

"Why shouldn't I be? What's it to do with me? You chase after stray trade if you like, but I've work to do."

This wasn't right. Not the hard edge to his voice, not the hard shell of not caring. This ought not be what Gil had become. Vikram loathed it, and that loathing pushed him to spit, "Selling pictures of people selling themselves."

"If I choose to," Gil said. "That's *my* trade. You don't like it, you know where the door is."

"No, I *don't* like it." Vikram had to shove the cat twice, violently, to detach it from his lap, and felt thread give way under its resisting claws. He stood, unreasonably but ferociously angry. "I don't like exploitation in any form. But what I really don't like is that you don't seem to give a damn for what appears to be a highly suspicious set of circumstances, and a young man missing, and the people who miss him."

Gil jabbed a finger at his own chest. "Bookseller. Not enquiry agent. You want one of those, there's a firm in Robin Hood Yard. What the devil do you think *I* can do?"

"I thought—"

I thought you might help me. It sounded absurd; it *was* absurd. As if Gil should drop everything to pursue Vikram's investigation as a matter of course. As if there were a reason to treat this man as anything more than a stranger. As if Gil would help Vikram now, when he hadn't so much as written a single line to get in touch.

Vikram should never have come to Holywell Street.

Chapter Four

Gil woke up the next day feeling uncomfortable.

He wasn't used to questioning his decisions. His life hadn't allowed him a great deal of leeway in making them, and the choices he'd made tended to be the kind that stuck. If you went around regretting things you might curl up and cry for the lost hopes and the ruined dreams, and bugger *that* for a game of tin soldiers. He was where he was. He did not need moralising, and he wasn't going to gaol.

That was not an option. He knew too much about the spirit-breaking pointless cruelty inflicted in Pentonville or Clerkenwell. He wasn't going to risk coming to the attention of the peelers for the sake of some boy he'd never met. Vikram could talk about the value of human life all he liked; he had education and wealth and doting parents to make his valuable. He could *afford* to care, and it was a bloody piece of cheek that he should ask Gil to do the same without a thought, as if it was the old days.

They'd initially palled up from sheer necessity as the only two dark-skinned boys in the form. It wasn't as though they'd had anything else in common. Gil was a housemaid's bastard, his mother's parents hauled over the seas by some fleshmongering son of a bitch. Vikram was rich and well born, and his father had been a high-up adviser to the government. Gil well recalled Vikram in a towering fury of offended pride that had made him seem older than his thirteen years, informing the entire common room that he was descended from princes. It hadn't been a good idea, as anyone could have advised him; he'd been dubbed 'Tippoo Sultan', not in a kindly spirit, ever after.

Vikram had always been proud. Probably no more so than the other boys, but a great deal more than most of them thought he had a right to be. He'd refused to be treated as second class, would not humble himself to be liked, and had paid the price in unpopularity.

He'd dropped the arrogance with Gil, though. Nobody could be alone all that time. They'd hidden themselves in dark corners of the school grounds, and Vik had huddled against him and talked, sometimes sobbed out the fears and unhappiness he couldn't push away, and...

They'd been friends. Real, deep friends, even if they were chalk and cheese, even if Gil couldn't see why Vik took everything so seriously and Vik couldn't see why Gil didn't. They'd been close, as close as it got.

And then Gil had left school that day in May, and he'd never seen Vikram again. He'd been busy, to say the least, learning to survive in a coldly hostile world, but he had still worried about his friend now and then. *What will he do without me?* he remembered thinking, as if he'd had time to worry about a clever, wealthy, beloved son. *How will he get on?*

Well, it looked like Vikram had got on just fine. Looked like he was making the world a better place, and was disappointed that Gil wasn't doing the same. *That was then, this is now. I run a dirty bookshop, mate,* Gil told him mentally. *What did you expect?*

The sod-you attitude had been carefully honed over years to serve him well as a suit of armour against family, moralisers, the law. People could hurt you far worse if you believed in them, or trusted them, or cared what they thought, so he'd learned to stop doing those things. He found himself not greatly wanting to stop them with Vikram.

"Oh, fuck off," he said aloud, to himself or whoever. He needed to forget about this whole thing, especially the angry, disappointed look in Vikram's eyes, and get on with some work. This meant another chapter of his current opus, *Miss Larch's School of Discipline.* Bums, whips, mock protests, schoolgirls, a young gentleman in a frock to tickle other fancies. He wanted to get that on sale before Christmas in a three-shilling edition.

Miss Larch was his priority, not a couple of tuppenny whores whose lives and deaths were none of his business. He repeated that to himself at twenty-minute intervals for the next two hours, slapped his pen down at last with a single scrawled sheet of uninspired vice to show for his time, and pushed his chair back with a snarl of, "Oh, all *right.*" He needed to finish with Matthew's collection anyway, and get those bloody photographs off his hands.

Upstairs, Satan slept on the chair Vikram had briefly occupied. Furry fuckster, curling up on Vik's thighs like he had a right to be there.

God, Vikram had got big. He'd been huge-eyed and slender that first day, when Gil had walked into the dormitory and seen the single brown-skinned boy staring back at him in the sea of pale faces, hostile or curious. He'd stayed awkward over the next seven years: gangly, thin-wristed, always hungry, as though he'd burned up the food with his intensity about everything under the sun. Even though he'd been starting to show a moustache by fourteen, he hadn't really started growing by the time they'd parted. Gil had tugged him around by the hand and Vik had let himself be dragged along.

Not that he'd been weak. Gil remembered his temper well. Exploding at the bullying and torment inflicted as a matter of course by larger boys on smaller; exploding at the taunts and sneers directed at his race or mother country; exploding at more or less anything that struck him as wrong, and a lot of things had. Opinionated pain in the arse, that was Vik as a schoolboy, and it looked like nothing much had changed on the inside. But the outside, though...

Hell's teeth, Vikram's outside was worth looking at these days. Eyes of such deep brown, with thick, straight black brows over them. Thick black hair, too, with a slight wave to it. The features that had always seemed too big for his face were still big—a beaky nose, a full mouth—but on a grown man, the effect was magnificent. And he'd filled out impressively in the shoulders, the very nice arse, and the thighs that bloody Satan had helped himself to, lying face down on Vikram's lap, when Gil could have cheerfully done the same.

Oh, Vikram grown up was a piece of work. And he was also a lawyer, and no matter what he said about his religion or philosophy, he was English by education. Gil would be well advised to keep within safe bounds. The last thing he needed was a moralising lawyer in his life, even one with thighs and eyes like those.

Gil wasn't looking for trouble and he definitely wasn't looking for Sunil as he sorted through Matthew's photographs. Men and women, orifices and the various things that might be stuck into them, the usual business over and over while the fog dragged dirty fingers across his windows and he tried not to remember being lost and sixteen.

It *wasn't* his problem, damn it. He'd never had Errol or wanted to. Gil didn't like young ones. Either they had eyes full of hope and need, and there was nothing Gil liked less than other people's need, or they'd had the optimism beaten out of them already, and that was just disheartening. He liked a man or woman who'd grown a thick skin with age, who was knocked down and got up and could laugh about it. Not people like, to pluck an example out of the air, Vikram, who cared so damn much about everything that it hurt to look at him, but those who could have a good time and not care and walk away unscathed. Because if you couldn't do that, you were in trouble.

Errol wouldn't be walking away, but there was nothing to be done for him now. The other one, Sunil, was probably dead too. These things happened. And just because they had maybe happened to two boys possibly on the same night...

It was none of his sodding business. Gil told himself that like a sensible purveyor of filth, but even so, once he'd finished going through the loose photographs, he decided he might as well take a look at the albums while he was at it.

By the time he'd got to the third one, he really was wondering about his half-brother.

Most people had their little ways, things they preferred—feet, or restraints, or floggers, or what-have-you. Matthew's collection had them all, and plenty more, and he'd organised them by theme. Orgy pictures together, cunnilingus pictures together, flogger pictures together, with spaces left for gaps, as though a pornographer had collided with a librarian. Someone was going to pay a fortune for these as a set, Gil had no doubt, but the overall effect was deathly in its monotony. Had Matthew really found pleasure in this organised catalogue of vice?

He picked up an album that still had a newish smell to it, opened it, and said, "Ah, *fuckery*."

It was Errol and Sunil. Of course it bloody was, in a run of six pictures of gamahuching and *soixante-neuf*. The photographic paper was clean and unblemished, and the prints sat in an album with an unfaded spine that a cursory flick showed to be two-thirds empty. These were very recent.

"Fuckery!" Gil said again, so loudly that Satan lifted his head and gave him a look of yellow-eyed hatred. "Well, now what?"

Satan yawned, revealing needlepoint teeth. Gil glared at him. "It's all right for you. Nobody's putting you to the crank if the peelers take an interest." Satan could fuck and murder as he pleased, and leave the bodies all over the shop floor too, frequently in pieces. Bloody cat.

What the devil was he to do now? He'd ignored a lot in his time. There was so much to ignore, after all, and if you went around caring about every beggar and every hungry child, you'd die of pity and do no good to anyone. He could ignore this: burn the pictures rather than risk questions, and searches, and a trip to gaol. Given Vikram's look of contempt as he'd left, he'd probably expect Gil to do just that, and Gil found a kind of bitter pleasure in fulfilling people's worst opinions. If they were going to judge him without knowing a damn thing about him, he might as well live down to their expectations. That had been a driving principle for years, and he wasn't going to change it for the sake of a half-remembered schoolboy friendship, or the disappointment in Vikram's eyes.

He was, therefore, really quite annoyed with himself as he stood in Vikram's offices in Lincoln's Inn an hour later, asking for Mr. Pandey.

Vik was wearing a black Newmarket coat over a pale grey waistcoat and dark grey trousers. He looked smart and decent and tired, and surprised. "Gil," he said blankly.

"Me. Can I have a word?"

"Come in."

Gil had never been in a law office before. It was very neat, dark wood and green leather, not at all the mess of Chancery papers he had in mind from reading Dickens.

"I didn't expect to see you," Vikram said. "I should probably apologise. I dare say I was unreasonable. I get caught up in things—well, you know that but—"

"I remember." Vikram's eyes were so bloody brown. Gil needed not to be lusting after a lawyer like this, let alone an old friend. "But, mate—"

"No, it wasn't reasonable. I had no right to expect you to take an interest in my work or my obligations, which are not yours."

That sounded like a well-used phrase. Possibly well used by someone else, to Vikram. "No, they aren't, but you need to see this."

Gil held out a photograph he'd extracted from the album. Vikram took it, and went rigid. "Sunil."

"The thing is, the other one's Errol," Gil said. "The boy I told you about. The one who was murdered."

"Is it. Is it indeed. Was this picture from your half-brother's collection?"

"Yes. I hate to say this, but you might have a point about the connection. Well, it's fishy as a six-day herring, but I still can't go to the police. And you can't take this to them and say where you got it, either."

Vikram's brows shot up. "Are you so concerned about your family name?"

"My name's Lawless. I couldn't give a monkey's for the Lawes."

"Then surely we can—"

Gil scrunched a handful of hair. "I could do time, Vik. You *know* that. There was this bloke had a shop a few doors down from mine, he got six months for sale of obscene publications. In Pentonville." Gil tried to say that casually, but Vikram's expression suggested he'd failed. Or maybe he just knew about Pentonville, and its solitary cells, and its silent system, and what it did to you as the endless weeks passed and you didn't speak to another human soul. "He did five and a half months, and hanged himself in his cell with a fortnight to go because he couldn't take another day." Or at least, that was what Gil imagined his reason to have been; that was what he'd dreamed about on several sweaty-cold nights afterwards, waking in a tangle of blankets. He didn't count himself a needy sort and, if asked, would have said he did fine on his own, but Pentonville gave him the screaming horrors.

"It doesn't sound fun," he said, not quite able to meet Vikram's eyes, not sure if it would be worse to see pity or contempt. "I don't fancy it myself."

"But you sell—"

"Plenty of legal goods," Gil cut in. "And nothing unlawful to people I don't know. I'm careful. But I'm known to the law all the same, and I can't just tell the police my half-brother left me a load of dirty pictures and expect them to take my word for it. It's not like the family will back me up."

"I understand." Vikram's brows were drawn together, forming a near-continuous thick black line. "But the provenance of the pictures might be important. I can't conceal it. That would be withholding evidence."

"Did you not hear me? If you say where you got these–"

"I heard you," Vikram said testily. "Let's compromise. I won't take any of this to the police yet, or do anything beyond what I have already, which is to report Sunil missing and put out his description to the authorities. But I will, I *must* look into this, and I need you to help me. You know this world. And if we find evidence of murder, I will do my best to present it in a way that doesn't involve you."

"But I have to help you, do I?"

"I need to find what happened to Sunil." Vikram's voice had an edge that you could have shaved with. It made Gil's skin prickle. "I *will* find that, with your help or that of the police. And don't tell me you don't care. You wouldn't have come here if you didn't care."

Gil wasn't entirely prepared to agree with that, but he decided not to argue. He'd liked Errol, for what that was worth, and he wouldn't mind spending a bit more time with Vik. So long as it was clearly understood he wasn't doing this out of the goodness of his heart.

He propped his arse against some bit of expensive, well-polished furniture, bumping a few papers off the top of a pile and making Vikram wince. "Right. What's your plan, then?"

"Just a moment. Can you give me a shilling?"

"What for?"

"You need to hire me as your solicitor. That way, I have professional privilege and I am not obliged to reveal anything you tell me. I don't say I shan't act on my own account if I see fit, of course."

"Nice for some. All right, here's your shilling."

Vikram took the coin he fished out. "Very well, you have a legal representative. I suggest we begin with your brother's collection. See if there are any other photographs of the boys and any indication of provenance. Who took them, who sold them."

"That'll take a while."

"You'd better start, then."

Gil broke out his best smile. "Going to give me a hand?"

"Looking at—?" Vikram's eyes widened. "No."

"You're my lawyer, aren't you? Don't I get legal help?"

"Looking at obscene materials is *not* part of a solicitor's obligations."

"Got anything better to do?"

"You think I have nothing better to do than look through pornographic images?" Vikram demanded.

"Well, you're here on a Saturday afternoon."

"Yes. I'm working. What else should I be doing?"

"Looking for Sunil, which'll be done twice as fast if you give me a hand. Oh, come on, we can catch up properly while we're about it. I'll buy you dinner."

"From your ill-gotten gains?"

Gil blinked at Vikram's tone. "Ah. That's it, is it?"

"What is?"

"You've really got a problem with the pictures?"

"Of course I do," Vikram snapped. "They're illegal, immoral, and obscene."

"Right, but what's bad about them? Come on, Vik, they're only pictures. People doing what people do."

"Illegally."

"You know I get magistrates in?" Gil said. "One fellow sent a bookseller on Wych Street downstairs for twelve months hard, and was in my place the week after, asking for flagellation stories. Law, my arse."

"People are flawed. That doesn't negate the rule of law."

"If flawed people invent laws, and flawed people apply 'em, what sort of law do you think you get?" Gil retorted. "Anyway, that's not the point. I'm not asking you to look at these for fun. I could use some help. And it *would* be good to catch up."

"Yes, but—" Vikram made an exasperated noise in his throat. "All right, curse you. Show me your filth."

Chapter Five

Vikram was not sure this was a good idea.

They had settled on the floor of Gil's upstairs room, since there was nowhere sensible to sit. Gil had thick rugs, at least, so Vikram's trousers would, he hoped, not be too ingrained with dust. Gil put three large leather-bound albums in front of him; Vikram squared his shoulders, and opened the first.

"Great Caesar's ghost," he muttered. "People buy these?"

The woman depicted had her legs up so her ankles were around her ears and was holding her private parts open with two fingers. It was not anything Vikram would have called erotic. Forbidden, without doubt, so forbidden that he had a queasy, nervous sensation looking at it, as he'd always had when Gil had dragged him into some piece of rulebreaking. But what he'd always been informed was the secret jewel of a woman's intimacy seemed to be, well, just hair and an asymmetrical sort of opening. People risked gaol to buy and sell this?

"Vik?" Gil was giving him a rather sardonic look. "We have a few of those to get through yet."

Vikram leafed through the album—all women—without comment and reached for the next. This one began with the image of a mostly naked man, still wearing socks and gaiters, as Sunil had been. He stood, skin ghostly pallid against what looked like a cloth backdrop, member hard and jutting and slightly darker than the rest of him. Flushed with blood, presumably. Vikram hadn't seen a white erection since his schooldays, and couldn't remember what they looked like in person.

"Got something?" Gil asked.

"No. Just... Nothing."

Gil cocked a meaningful brow. Vikram glared. "You can't expect me to take this sort of thing in my stride. Really, Gil, why do you do it?"

"What, sell this stuff? Money."

"There are other things to sell."

"Yeah, books," Gil said. "To be honest, that's mostly my line. I'm not a photograph man, certainly not on this scale."

That was something of a relief. Pornographic books would still incur gaol time, but he'd rather know Gil traded in imagination than images. "But why this business in general?" Vikram asked. "What *happened*? You were doing perfectly well at school, and then your father died, and then you were gone!"

"They really didn't say?"

"Nothing!" Vikram's voice betrayed the outrage he still felt to an embarrassing degree. "Nobody told me anything. You vanished, with all your things. The masters said you'd been withdrawn from school, and refused to tell me why. I wrote to Wealdstone House a dozen times and never had a reply."

"No, you wouldn't have." Gil leafed through a few more pictures, as though that was all there was to say, and then sat back on his heels. "All right, you want to know? Well, my father died. I was sent back to school after the funeral while they did the legal business and Matthew got his feet under the table. And then he wrote to the school, told them he wanted me removed right away. And he was head of the family and paid the bills, so out I went."

"But *why*?"

"Because he didn't like my face," Gil said flatly. "He didn't even tell me in person that he'd be kicking my feet from under me, just sent his man of business, Vilney, to the school to do it. 'You're sixteen years old and have lived on the family's generosity long enough,' he said. 'It's time for you to take responsibility for yourself. Oh, and if you show your face at Wealdstone House again, Mr. Lawes will have you whipped.' And there I was."

"But did your father not leave you anything to live on?"

"Oh, yes. He left me ten pounds."

"What?"

"Vilney gave me a banknote," Gil said, with a sour smile. "He said that was the last I'd see of Lawes money, that I'd leeched off the estate long enough."

Vikram stared at him. "But... Ten pounds? Your father—" His throat closed. He knew stories like that, every solicitor did. People could be astonishingly cruel, or thoughtless, in their wills. But Gil had adored his father. The compulsory letter home had been a pleasure for him each week, not a chore, and *my father says* had been his clincher to any argument. Vikram had always believed the love to be reciprocated. He didn't want to imagine the pain of that callous blow, how much it would hurt even now, what the little sardonic smile on Gil's face must cost him.

"Dear heaven, Gil. I don't know what to say. But what did you do?" He was gripping the photograph album tightly, he realised. He set it on the rug. "Where did you go? Why didn't you write?"

"Yes, well." Gil shrugged carelessly, but he wasn't meeting Vikram's eyes. "Look, one moment I had a father, and the next he was dead and it turned out he hadn't given a damn for me. Hadn't thought me worth looking after, didn't care if I lived or died. And I'd always known my brother loathed me but to find out he wouldn't even let me finish my schooling, or at least find somewhere to go first, that he *wanted* me beggared–" His words were accelerating now, tumbling out. "And I'd been at that school seven years, boarding, living there more than half the damned year, and the headmaster told me to pack my trunk in half an hour and be off the premises. I asked him where I was to go–I was crying, Vik, I couldn't stop, I was so afraid–and he looked at his hands and muttered about it not being his concern."

"Gil–"

"I was in a history lesson that morning, and on the road with a ten-pound note to my name that night. By the next morning I'd been robbed of everything but the clothes I slept in. I went from schoolboy to vagrant in one day, and nobody on earth cared. Nobody cared."

"I did," Vikram said hoarsely. "My parents would have helped if I'd asked them. I'm sure of it."

"Yes, and I was sure my father would have left me something to live on, but that didn't happen either, did it? I was sixteen. My father was dead, my whole life had been turned–not even upside down, worse than that. Thrown on the dustheap. I couldn't think what to do; I couldn't think at all for the shock. And maybe if I'd had a bit of time to come to grips with everything I might have gone back to school, found a way to send in a note to you or suchlike, but– Well. That didn't happen."

Vikram didn't like the note in his voice. "What did happen?"

Gil shrugged again. "Like I say, I got robbed. I had nothing to eat and one thing to sell."

Vikram didn't understand that for a moment, and then he felt a chill of unpleasant anticipation. "What do you mean?" he made himself ask.

"If you must know, I was sucking pricks for shillings within a couple of days."

Vikram tried to control his expression. He obviously failed because Gil's chin went up. "It was that or stealing and I was a bit obvious for that out in the countryside, even if I'd had any knack for it. Whereas I probably got a bit of extra business off gentlemen by being a novelty. Like your lad Sunil."

Vikram felt nausea rise. "You shouldn't have had to do that. You *shouldn't.*"

"Yeah, well." Gil jerked a hand at the photographs in front of him. "You don't like these pictures? I can tell you, a warm dry studio is a lot more fun than a wet alley, and easier on the knees."

"Stop."

"It's what happened. It's what Matthew reduced me to, just another bit of dirt on the streets, like he thought I always was. And if you're going to tell me that I should have run to your parents, turned up in rags at their beautiful clean house and asked to live there—well. Maybe they'd have welcomed me with open arms, but nobody else was doing that, so why would I think they might?"

"Dear heaven. I don't know what to say."

"Start with 'Matthew Lawes was a lying cunt'," Gil said. "My father left me five hundred pounds down and fifty a year for life. My brother cheated me out of my inheritance."

"*What?*" Vikram almost shouted.

"I didn't know that then, of course. Didn't begin to suspect. That fucker Vilney could lie his way through a brick wall."

"But–"

"Illegal, fraud, I know. Let me get this damn fool story finished first, will you? I made my way to London the best I could, and it wasn't much of a laugh for a couple of years trying to keep afloat. There's a lot of people trying to make a crust in this city. And then I met a bloke who put me in the way of a bit of work for William Dugdale. Ever hear of him?"

"I suppose you don't mean the seventeenth-century antiquary."

"I mean the pornographer. Sold more dirt than a nightsoil company. He was a dodgy swine, always in and out of gaol, and a rotten plagiarist as well, but he offered me a bit of work fetching and carrying, and then once he realised I had a decent education, he gave me more to do. Sorting books, selling 'em, then writing. I learned the ropes, and helped keep things running when he got hauled off to chokey for the last time. He died in sixty-eight in the Clerkenwell House of Correction, poor bastard. They wouldn't let him have books or writing materials in there, and it sent him off his rocker. He didn't even recognise his daughter at the last. Anyway, he was dead, and I was just wondering what to do next when Percy caught up with me."

"Percy– Percival Lawes? Your cousin?" Vikram remembered a younger, eager boy, all enthusiasm and hero-worship.

"He'd started as a clerk at Somerset House, where they do the public records. He looked up Pa's will one day, out of idleness. Matthew had told him that I hadn't been left anything, but there it was in black and white. Percy tracked me down to tell me."

Vikram nodded, feeling the bitter stab of self-rebuke, almost resentment. If Percival Lawes, who was in his recollection entirely negligible, had found Gil, Vikram could have done the same. If he had *looked,* if he hadn't given up after that last search and accepted Gil was dead rather than endure the pain of him missing, he might have been there when Gil had needed him.

"Good old Percy," he said as sincerely as he could. "Good man."

"He's all right. Better than the rest of them. Not hard to be better than Matthew, mind you."

"And then what? Did you prosecute?"

Gil shook his head. "Matthew said he and Vilney would swear in court that I'd refused the money, and he'd fight it all the way. I didn't think it was worth trying."

"He committed a crime!"

"And nobody ever gets away with that." Gil scrubbed a hand in his hair. "Maybe I could have prosecuted, but I didn't think I could risk losing in court and being stuck with solicitor's fees. I got him to hand over my lump sum and start paying the fifty a year from then on. No interest or the missed payments, though, he wouldn't admit to owing that."

"You should have had it."

"I should have, yes, when I needed it. And I shouldn't have needed it. If Matthew hadn't set out to make me go away, I don't suppose I'd be in Holywell Street now. But there you are. I could have ended up a lawyer in a good suit if things had been different—Lawless and Pandey or whatever—and I could have ended up like Errol, and there's no point thinking about it, because none of that's going to change."

"But once you had the lump sum, once you had financial independence, you nevertheless decided to stay in this line?"

"Why not? It was what I knew. And..." He paused for long enough that Vikram wondered if he'd go on at all, then spoke quietly. "Matthew took my father from me. I was sixteen and my pa was dead, and Matthew told me he'd never given a damn for me, and I believed it. Years, I believed it. Everything I had to do to survive because Pa hadn't cared about me, all the time I'd spent thinking the sun shone whenever he spoke and he hadn't cared a bit—I hated my father for that, Vik. I hated him more than I hated Matthew. And it wasn't true. It was a miserable lie, but I believed it for so long that it still *feels* true. I can't forget what I felt. I said Matthew had turned my life upside down, didn't I? Well, finding out he was a liar didn't turn it the right way up again. It didn't make things better."

"No. I see."

"My brother stole my father from me to save himself fifty pounds a year," Gil said. "And he did it with the help of his man of business and a good family of English gentlemen—because Jessamy and Horace would have been there when the will was read. They *knew*. They knew he was cheating me and they didn't care. So fuck them. Fuck the lot of them. I took this shop because to hell with English gentlemen, and the law, and the done thing, and the kind of respectability that means keeping other people in line while you do as you please. I took the shop to show I'd survive—no, *thrive*, whatever they did, and I put my name on it because I thought it might piss Matthew off all the more to be associated with filthy books. Ha. I missed the mark there, didn't I? Anyway, that's that." He gave a little shrug, not the usual easy don't-care movement, more as if trying to knock some crawling thing off his shoulder without touching it. "That's why I left school like I did, and it's why I didn't get in touch afterwards. Because what part of any of that would you have wanted to hear?"

"'I'm alive'," Vikram said. "I wanted to hear that. It's all that matters. I'm so sorry, Gil."

Gil's eyes met his. They were a shade lighter than his skin, brown with amber depths, and just for a moment they were wide and raw and unguarded, and Vikram wanted to reach out and pull him close. He wanted to hold Gil until that damned hard shell of his shivered away and he felt the boy he used to know, the one who would grab on and hold tight and laugh through tears, telling him everything would be fine.

Gil didn't look like he thought everything would be fine ever again.

But Vikram didn't reach for him, because he didn't know how, and Gil looked away. He picked up a photograph album as though it were interesting, and said, quite casually, as though they'd discussed nothing but the weather, "So what about you?"

"What? Me?" Vikram couldn't seem to understand the question.

"While I was off making a living. What did you do with yourself?"

"Oh. Uh. I went up to Oxford, to read law."

"How was that?"

Vikram had absolutely no desire to speak about himself now, but Gil could hardly make his wishes clearer. "Er, busy. I got involved in politics."

"I bet you did. Indian independence?"

"And the rights of Indians living here. The way that Indian workers are treated is a disgrace. Lascars are paid a pittance and left to starve; ayahs are brought over and abandoned. Someone needs to speak for them."

"And that's you, is it? What do your parents think to that?"

"We, ah, we aren't on marvellous terms at the moment. They find me rather disappointing."

Gil's brows slanted. "Must have high standards. What happened?"

"Well, they disagree with my political views. And my choice of career. And my choice of clients. Everything, really. My father wanted me to be a barrister and aim for Parliament. To work at a higher level, not to spend my time in the gutters of Shad Thames. And then there was the trip to India."

Gil sat up. "Blimey. What was that like?"

Vikram picked the next photograph off the pile, glaring at it. "I didn't go."

"Sorry?"

"I have work here, people who need me, and it's a damned long way. It would take months I couldn't spare."

Gil blinked. "Have you ever gone?"

"No. I... No. It was never convenient."

"But you always said you wanted to go home as soon as you'd finished school. You talked about it all the time."

"I know. I wanted to complete my studies at Oxford first, though, and then I was offered a pupillage right away, you see, and–" Gil was listening with his head cocked, a very familiar gesture of sceptical enquiry. Vikram felt himself sag. "Well, it's not that easy. India is my homeland, but we came here when I was three. My parents always spoke English at home. I don't speak anything except English and French."

"I'm sure you could find someone to translate."

"Of course, but– Look, I'm an Indian national. That's important to me. I count myself an Indian, not an Englishman."

"So?"

"So what if I went home and didn't feel as though I belonged?" Vikram blurted the words. "If 'home' wasn't home at all, what–who–would I be then? What if I was an Englishman there?"

It was almost a relief to say the words out loud when he'd barely articulated the thought to himself previously. It had always been easy to talk to Gil. "You don't have to tell me that's absurd," he added, in case. "I'm sure it sounds ridiculous."

"It doesn't," Gil said. "There's nothing funny about having your roots torn up. Thinking you belong somewhere and the people there don't agree."

Vikram's lungs felt tight. "It's not the same. Of course it's not."

Gil ignored that. "But I don't know if it wouldn't be worth taking the risk. You always wanted to go."

"I did. But the longer I waited the harder it seemed, and...well, I haven't gone, that's all."

"Maybe you need to make it all a bit less meaningful. Just a visit, without looking for a homeland."

"I'm not very good at making things less meaningful," Vikram pointed out, and won a quick grin that helped his muscles relax just a fraction.

"Fair point. How about this: if you went to India, you might even see the sun again."

"Now, that is a compelling argument. Damn this sodden island."

"I vote you book a berth right now, and take one for me while you're at it."

"That's a bargain."

They exchanged quick smiles. Vikram returned to the photographs, rather hoping that they would leave the subject here, but Gil spoke again after a moment.

"So your parents aren't happy you haven't gone?"

Vikram contemplated the photograph he held. "Not at all, no. They took it really quite badly. I hadn't understood it mattered to them so much, but they seem to feel I've turned my back on my heritage, which, considering they made their own home here and chose this country in which to bring me up–" He could hear his voice rising, and stopped himself. "Well, it's not worth going over. The long and short of it is that I was angry with myself for letting them down, and with them for expecting more, or different, from me, and we argued quite badly. It's been awkward since."

"It would be." Gil didn't say anything else, didn't point out how damned lucky Vikram was to have loving, even if disagreeing, parents. Vikram wondered whether he knew it didn't need saying, or if he just didn't care.

Silence fell after that. It was almost a relief. Vikram hadn't spoken so honestly to anyone in a very long time, and he suspected Gil was in much the same boat. It was as though they'd picked up their friendship at the point it had been broken thirteen years ago and slipped back into intimacy without thought, leaving them both now unsettled and exposed.

They carried on working. Vikram leafed through the album he held, image after image of intimate parts, breasts and pudenda, pale flesh and tangled limbs, all dishearteningly similar. He found himself rapidly more intrigued by the bizarre variety of backgrounds than the depravity. Some images had painted backdrops showing thatched cottages and countryside, occasionally for bucolic scenes with costumes, sometimes for no apparent reason at all. An orgy was backed with painted Roman-type columns. Where drapes were used, most were plain, but a few had patterns, including a truly strange one with giant flowers. He took up the next album, expecting much the same, and stopped dead.

All the ones so far had been women, or men and women. This was two men, both rampantly erect, facing one another against thick drapes of a dark colour.

The next showed the same pair, one now on his knees, the other with a hand on his shoulder. In the third, the kneeling man had the other's stiff piece in his mouth.

In his *mouth.* Lips closed around it almost to the base, even though it was surely far too big for that. Vikram felt as though he had something in his own throat. He swallowed, turned the page. One man sprawled back on a divan that had been added to the scene, legs wide. The other leaned over so that each had his mouth close to the other's stand.

In the next–

"I can't do this." Vikram pushed the album away. "I'm sorry."

"Why, what's wrong with it?" Gil squinted over, frowning.

"It's illegal. The image, and the act. I can't have anything to do with it."

"Well, yes. Though, if it helps, I know these two." Gil indicated the photograph. The man on hands and knees, legs wide, the other behind him. "They aren't doing anything they wouldn't be doing on their day off, trust me. And they were both alive last Wednesday, in case you're worried."

Vikram hadn't even considered that. It was the least of his problems. "I just don't want to look at these, that's all."

Except that he'd promised he would, he'd promised to help. Except that he did want to look at them. Or rather he didn't, but he did.

Gil cocked his head. "Well, if it's not your cup of tea, fair enough. But it's just people doing what people do. Human nature, whatever the law says."

"The law holds that it's unnatural."

"The law holds that India belongs to Britain."

"That's not the law– That's not the *point*– Oh, great Scott, Gil, does none of this mean anything to you?" He gestured, knocking a pile of prints stacked on the rug. They slid sideways, fanning like a deck of cards, revealing glimpses of bare legs, buttocks, bodies.

"A tidy profit. What else should it mean?"

"Why do you need the money? You have your inheritance, don't you?"

Gil's eyes hardened. "Try something for me, Vik. Try having everything kicked out from under you and being left with nothing, and then ask me why I don't fancy it happening again."

"Granted, but *this*–"

"What's so wrong with it?"

"I don't approve of the exploitation of unfortunates." Vikram didn't want to consider Gil all those years ago, forced to do these things by men who used the poor for pennies. He wanted to scrub the feel of the prints from his fingers. "Or the licentiousness and self-indulgence that went into their creation."

"Self-indulgence," Gil said. "You mean fun?"

"I don't indulge in that sort of 'fun'," Vikram said through his teeth.

"Well, you used to, as I recall."

It knocked the breath out of him. Vikram stared at the floor, the photographs, because looking at Gil would be worse. "That wasn't what I meant. I was referring to the, the purchasers of these images, not the act, which, which isn't– We were boys. It's irrelevant."

"Right, got you. But since you mention it, yes, we were boys, and we had fun, and we didn't do each other any harm. You don't have to tie yourself in knots about it."

"I am not tying myself in knots."

"You've been tying yourself in knots your whole life. I've not seen you in thirteen years, and I can tell you haven't changed a bit. You need to loosen some of those before you strangle yourself."

And there it was, at last, Vikram's best friend: anger, rushing through him and pushing everything else back. "You can't tell anything about me. You don't know me because, as you so rightly say, it's been thirteen years. I don't need to take your advice; I do very well as I am. And I will not sit here amid filth being mocked because I don't choose to soil myself with it. You can call it tying myself in knots. I call it principles."

"Fine. All right," Gil said. "Jesus, mate, calm down."

Vikram rose. "I am perfectly calm. I need some fresh air."

"Well, you won't get it round here."

Vikram ignored that, scooping up his coat and hat. Gil said something as he left but he didn't listen, clattering down the stairs, needing to be outside.

It was dark already, and there was a light fog. It would get a great deal worse as they slipped into winter, but it was already enough to catch in his throat as he strode up and down Holywell Street, trying not to tread in anything nasty.

How dare Gil? How dare he presume to comment on Vikram's principles, how dare he assume that Vikram ought to follow in his footsteps through the mire? How could he be so casual about it considering the horrors of his own past, let alone their shared experience? How dare he speak as though it were easy?

We had fun, and we didn't do each other any harm.

Evidently it had done Gil no harm. He had not been remotely affected. Vikram was quite surprised he even remembered, given how very trivial and unimportant their *fun* had apparently been. Curse Gil, curse all of it. Those pictures, those two men, hands and mouths and worse.

Gil had used his hands. Vikram remembered that very clearly indeed.

They'd been fifteen, the two of them, and inseparable. No longer just allies in that miserable school, but friends. They partnered in study where they were in the same class, in games wherever possible, and Gil knew every nook and cranny in the school where they could slip away to experiment with cheroots, to play cards, to talk about everything and anything and nothing. They shared fears and hopes, idle dreams, fantasies and injuries. They squabbled and laughed, comforted each other after the casual cruelties and beatings, and then...

They'd been on the roof. You could get up there and sit behind the parapet, away from prefects and bullies and masters alike, looking out at the countryside around. It had felt like freedom. They'd been talking about one of the sixth-formers who it was said had been sacked for immorality. Leaning back together, on the slates, Gil pillowing his head casually on Vikram's outstretched arm, looking at him.

I don't even know what immorality he was up to, Vikram had said. *Nobody tells me anything.* And Gil had given that rich laugh of his, already deepening, and said, *Want to find out?*

Of course Vikram had known. You couldn't avoid it in a school packed with boys growing to manhood, where privacy was hard come by. He'd heard boys breathing in the night, in the dorm room; he knew about the prefects one should always visit in pairs.

He'd asked anyway, and when Gil returned his invitation, he'd said yes.

That first time it had been a matter of following instructions. *Unbutton your fly. Give it a rub.* And then Gil's hand, so impossibly warm and soft, touching him, Gil smiling as though there could be nothing more natural and enjoyable, and Vikram had stared up at the sky and felt his heart bursting along with his balls.

Gil's hand. Vikram could feel the blood pounding now.

Gil had never fretted. Where Vikram edged his way through the narrow space left for him by morals, expectations, obligations, fear of consequences, and pride, Gil strolled freely. He hadn't cared if what they were doing was wrong in other people's eyes; he'd done it because he thought it a good thing to do, and Vikram had felt his own world expanding too. Gil shoving him into the games cupboard for swift, frantic rutting; Gil reaching over the narrow gap between their beds in the dark of the dormitory.

He'd just been a schoolboy, urgent with the seething needs of growing youth. Everyone did it, by themselves or with a particular friend or with half the school. Of course Gil hadn't cared, even if it had felt like that at the time. But Vikram had. He'd cared so much it seemed to fill up all the gaps in his mind, like water poured into a jar full of stones. He'd felt his trammelled existence opening out like the sky over the school roof, felt his awkward, growing body and mind and heart come into alignment because of course it was easy with Gil. Everything was.

And then Gil had disappeared one day, somewhere between breakfast and bedtime, and nothing had ever been easy again.

Chapter Six

Gil wasn't sure if Vikram was going to come back in, and was unreasonably relieved when he heard footsteps on the stairs. He wouldn't have gone running after him, that would be stupid, but nobody would want an old mate to walk off in a huff like that for no reason.

Or if there had been a reason it was the tension of their prior conversation, those painful revelations spilled out to someone who was and wasn't a stranger, was and wasn't a friend. Doubtless Vikram hadn't wanted to be reminded of their youthful misdeeds. There were plenty of men who started regretting their acts thirty seconds after they spent; of course it would be embarrassing for an upright lawyer to recall his schoolboy passions, and how very much they'd seemed to mean at the time.

Vikram didn't make any reference to their conversation or his abrupt disappearance when he came back in. He just hung up his coat in the corner again, and Gil took a look at him while he did so. A lot of his height was in his legs, which had the lean look of someone who walked a lot. Come to that, his expensive shoes were heavily worn on the sole though the uppers were smartly polished. Vikram wasn't the sort to sit in a hackney when he could be striding along the pavement.

Vikram knelt back down to the pictures, his expression closed. Controlled, it was; controlled enough to make Gil wonder what he was controlling.

They'd played the fool as boys, and it had been...more than fun. It had seemed important then, overwhelming at times. It was hard to imagine that now, these many years over the chasm that separated Gil's adulthood from his boyhood; hard to remember any of the things that had seemed so important when he'd had things to take for granted, like a soft bed and food and a father who loved him. If Matthew's malice hadn't pulled the pair of them apart—

Well, who knew. Maybe Gil would have been the first one to break Vikram's heart. He was glad he hadn't done that.

Vikram had come to the end of an album, so Gil passed him another. He groaned. "How much of this is there?"

"Shelves. Matthew liked his pictures."

"I can't say I feel the same."

"Yes, but you don't enjoy much."

Vikram's head came up sharply. His eyes looked huge, dark and liquid, and Gil felt like a shit. It was the kind of dig he'd been used to making when things were different. "Sorry. Look, you don't have to like pictures. You don't have to like anything. All I meant was, uh." He stalled on that.

"What did you mean?"

Gil sighed. "Look, if you don't like fucking, that's fine. And if you like it, that's fine too. It's all fine if you're happy. It's just, you don't look happy."

"You don't know me."

"No, I don't, you're right. Fair enough. *Are* you happy?"

Vikram blinked. It looked like a question he hadn't expected to be asked. "I...have a fulfilling, busy life."

"That's not what I asked. I'm not trying to give you a hard time, Vik. I just think, if there's something you want, you might as well try to have it. Everyone else does."

"I'm a lawyer. I know what *everyone else* does because it frequently brings them into court. And what do you mean, something I want?"

Gil put down the photograph he held. "What I mean is, I don't see any harm in taking pleasure with people who choose to take it with you. That's all."

"Yes, but these people"—he waved a photograph—"didn't choose."

"You don't know that," Gil pointed out. "I've met plenty of people in this line of work. They aren't all victims, and you don't get to treat them like tragedies."

"But if people are forced to this degradation by financial need—"

"Like I was," Gil filled in for him. "Yes, that happens. Life's hard. Does that mean I never get to enjoy myself again?"

"Great Scott, Gil, how can you treat this so lightly?"

"Why do you carry everything so heavy? What's wrong with saying, 'I'll do as I please, as long as it pleases whoever I'm with'?"

"And doesn't that matter? Don't you care who you're with? Isn't that important?" Vikram's lips were thin with tension.

A small voice at the back of Gil's mind was nagging at him, pointing out how much of a disaster this conversation could become. If Vikram walked out again— But he wasn't going to walk out, Gil was sure. And it was his Vik, right here, after thirteen years, still weighted down by too much thinking. Gil had spent years of his youth trying to get that expression off Vikram's face. He looked so much better laughing.

"What's important," he said carefully. "For me, what's important is that you give each other a good time when you can. Carpe diem, as they used to say at school. Take your pleasures where you find them, while they last."

"And do anything you like, because it doesn't really matter?"

"Being alive matters," Gil said, on a sudden wave of something like anger. "It matters that I've got a warm room and a full belly, and I know that because I went a while without those things, which I'll bet is more than you ever did. It matters that I've a pal with me, and there's something I reckon you've been missing. It matters to be happy instead of miserable."

"You can be all those things without—" Vikram gestured at the photographs.

"True, you can. Or you can be them *with*, and have a lot of fun that way. Fine if that's not what you want, but if it *is* what you want, what good is it to pretend you don't? Who's that helping?"

"It's not that easy," Vikram said. His eyes were locked on Gil's now. So deep, so dark, so revealing. How could Vik be a lawyer, telling lies to judge and jury, when Gil could look into his eyes and see everything?

"It's as easy as you want it to be." *It was easy for us before*, Gil almost said, and didn't. Something had changed since before, if only that they were older, and worn, and Vikram's youthful enthusiasm was weighted by all the legal, moralising bollocks people let the world put on their shoulders. "Look—" He leaned forward. Vik stiffened, almost flinching, his crouch suddenly seeming more like a hunch, and Gil thought, *Ah, hell.*

He came round, stepping over the spread of photographs, and knelt by Vikram's side, putting a hand on his shoulder, in a way that he was sure couldn't be read as anything but comfort. "It's only me. Look, ignore me. I just thought—forget it." The tension in Vikram's shoulder made it solid under Gil's hand. Christ, was he frightened or something? "Don't be a neddy. Nobody's making you do anything you don't want."

"The issue is not that I don't want anything," Vikram said through his teeth. "That is not the issue at all."

Gil hadn't thought it was. He was beginning to feel he'd splashed into waters a great deal too deep for comfort. "Well, then..." Well then what? He was entirely unsure how to extricate them both from this conversation, or if that was even what Vikram needed him to do. "Christ's sake. Is there anything you don't make difficult?"

"No."

Gil spluttered, and Vikram's shoulders gave a single responsive shake. He said, sounding a little less tense, "I don't take things casually."

"Course not."

"And you don't take things seriously."

"Not so much. You'll break your heart that way."

"I remember that," Vikram said, very softly. "I remember not taking things seriously, and I liked it. Everything seems such a responsibility now."

"I tell you what, the world would be a better place with more like you," Gil said. "There's nothing wrong with being responsible. But you aren't responsible for me." He put his free hand out, his right arm crossing over his body to cover Vik's right hand, felt the tension in the strong, slim fingers, and a shiver of response. "Look, do what you want, and nothing that you don't.

Only–" To say this, or not? What if he did, and Vik took the hump? What if he didn't, and Vik went off in this seething state of wanting he didn't seem to understand? Men got in trouble that way when they plunged into a world of which they didn't know the rules. Gil didn't like to think of Vikram's desires becoming a danger, not when that could be avoided.

Right, so any approach would simply be a safety precaution. Who was he trying to fool?

God damn it. They were grown men. He'd say it outright and Vikram could do as he chose. "Look, mate, it's simple enough. If you feel like a bit of fun, like we used to, you know where to come. That's all."

"If I– Why?" That wasn't an aggressive demand. It was almost a whisper.

"Ah, come on. You must know you're fit as a butcher's dog. Or maybe you don't, but you can take my word for it. You grew up well."

"Taller than you," Vikram said, with an effort at a smile.

"Rub it in, why don't you." Gil pressed the hand he held. It was meant to be a friendly gesture, maybe a comforting one, but Vikram's fingers flattened under Gil's, inviting more pressure, and Gil pressed his own hand down harder, sliding his fingers between Vikram's, feeling the shape of the slender bones. Vikram swallowed audibly. Gil pushed a little harder, and then again, press and release, setting up a familiar rhythm, and heard Vikram's breath quicken.

He probably shouldn't be doing this. Vikram was a bundle of rigidity knotted by nerves. But he was also sodding lovely to look at, with those bottomless eyes and the curve of his lips, fulfilling a promise that his awkward boyhood hadn't offered, and mostly he was Vik. It *felt* right, that was all, even though a part of Gil's mind was telling him it really probably wasn't.

Well, if he'd listened to that part of his mind much, he wouldn't be where he was now. Of course, that was in Holywell Street, but this still felt right, so he increased the pressure, flexing his hand over Vik's as though he was touching something a lot more sensitive, and watched his lips part and move in silence, his eyes half-shut.

He still had a hand on Vik's shoulder. He ran it up, into that thick hair, fingers over the scalp, and felt Vik's head come back, pushing into his palm. He had a bloody nice throat, strong, slender-boned, the Adam's apple not too pronounced. Gil would have liked to get his mouth to that but who knew if that would send Vik into a panic. He couldn't recall if they'd used to kiss as boys, or work out if Vik would want that; some men recoiled at stubble, or intimacy.

Vik didn't look like he'd fear intimacy now. His mouth was open now, his eyes shut, his breath hot and hard– Christ, he looked like he was going to spend from having his hand touched, just from the pleasure of that rhythmic pressure, and Gil wanted to see Vik come more than he could recall wanting anything in years. He was poker-hard himself just from kneading another fellow's hand, or from the promise, the awareness, the feel of Vik's skin under his.

Vik wouldn't appreciate dealing with the mess after, if he spent fully clothed. Never comfortable, a bit embarrassing, and indignity was probably not something Vik laughed off easily. Which meant Gil really ought to take things in hand. As it were.

"Vik," he murmured. "Can I touch you?"

Vikram nodded, but his fingers closed urgently around Gil's. Gil shifted himself awkwardly sideways and round to face him, bringing his free hand down, and trailed it over Vikram's shirt front. Vikram inhaled desperately, a little panicked gasp.

Christ above. When was the last time anyone had laid a hand on him?

This was unnerving. Gil wasn't used to inexperience, and didn't like it. He'd hardly ever fucked anyone who didn't know what they were doing, and on the couple of occasions he had, they'd been eager to learn.

Vikram didn't look eager. He looked—Gil wasn't even sure how he looked. Like a sacrifice. Like a statue. Like the loveliest thing Gil had set eyes on in a long time, like a well-off lawyer with a rock-hard cockstand, like Gil's best friend who didn't quite know what was going on.

"Fuck," Gil said aloud. "Vik?"

Vikram opened his eyes. They were strained, and dizzy, and hungry, so hungry. Gil waited till they met his. "Mate," he said, and heard the thickness of his own voice. "I need to know you want this."

Vikram nodded, a tiny movement. "I— Yes. But Gil, could you, could we..."

Gil hoped he was more articulate in the courtroom. "I'll do anything you want if you tell me what it is. I don't read minds."

"I, uh..." Vikram hesitated a second more, face tense with uncertainty, and then he leaned forward and got his mouth to Gil's. You couldn't call it a kiss, exactly, with noses in the wrong places and faces at the wrong angles, but that was what he was going for, and Gil shifted into it to get it right, and—

Of course they'd used to kiss at school. Of course they had, when he'd shoved Vik backwards into a cupboard or a dark corner and they'd frotted against each other, mouths locked, all sweat and spit and spending. The familiarity swept over him in a dizzy rush, like he'd stood up too fast after a few too many gins, and the urgent, startled grunt in Vikram's throat suggested he wasn't the only one falling on his face in Memory Lane.

Gil grabbed for him, felt Vikram's hands on his waist, hauled him backwards so they were sprawling on the floor. They kissed frantically, Vikram's mouth gaining confidence, his body heavy in all the wrong places as if he wasn't aware that a man's weight on another fellow's groin could put quite a crimp in proceedings. Gil shoved and rolled till they were both on their sides, and got his hands to Vikram's waistband. Vikram was gasping and panting and kissing, and very definitely all right with this, and Gil worked his hand through cloth to the hard, ridged length of Vik's stiff prick...and stopped. Just stopped, so they were lying body to body, mouth to mouth, hand to cock, like that one desperately daring night when he'd come to Vikram's house in the holidays and crept into his room and his bed.

God, he'd been happy then.

They were both still, holding the quivering, silent moment, and then Gil curled his fingers around Vikram's stand, gave it a long stroke. Vikram made a noise of agony, so Gil did it again, this time running his thumb over the head, caressing every inch, and Vikram groaned as he came, thrusting in Gil's hand.

They lay together a moment longer as Vikram's shoulders heaved. Gil's own cock felt like an unpricked sausage sizzling in a pan, about to burst out of its skin. He gritted his teeth against the urge to do something about it.

Vikram's eyes fluttered open. Gil watched his face as he gently disengaged his wet hand, saw his weak smile.

"You all right?"

"You haven't changed at all," Vikram said. "Have you? You can still wrap me round your little finger."

Well, that was that, then. Gil began to sit up. Vikram tugged him down. "No, stop. I didn't mean that as a rebuke. I—Great Scott, Gil."

"Are you going to start worrying about things?" Gil asked, somewhat warily.

Vikram shook his head, then added, "Or, I shall try not to, at least. But that... Oh, the devil." He put his hand out, tentatively, to Gil's arm. "I missed you so much. It was all so easy, and it all seemed so right, and then you vanished. And I've never—with anyone—since, because it seemed so hard after that, so—"

"Whoa. Wait. You haven't fucked since *school*?"

"I haven't—" Vikram supplied the verb with a slight motion of his hand "—since you. You are the sum total of my experience, I'm afraid."

Gil attempted to get himself round that. "You've never fucked *anyone*? In thirteen years?" Vikram shook his head, flushing slightly. "Sweet King Jesus!"

"It's hardly that unusual." Vikram sounded a little nettled. "I'm not married, I don't choose to exploit unfortunates, and I don't want the clap. So I exercise self-control. Except just now."

Oh, no, no. He'd lived like a priest of Rome, or whatever the Hindu equivalent might be, for all those years, a model of virtue and self-restraint, and he'd just let Gil toss him off on the dusty floor of a dirty bookshop?

God in heaven. Gil could almost feel the appalling burden of responsibility sliding from Vikram's shoulders to his own. He knew what he'd say to another man or woman. *That was a laugh. Nice to have a frolic. Catch you round and about sometime.* He couldn't say that to Vikram, but dear Christ and all his angels, what the fuck *was* he supposed to say or do, knowing he was Vikram's one and only? The panic closed his throat for a second. Gil didn't look after other people: he looked after himself because that was how you survived when everyone else let you down and threw you away, and he had no idea at all what to do now.

He needed to give some sort of answer. If only he had one to give.

"Well. That's...well... Bugger me, Vik, I don't know what to say. If you want to pretend that didn't happen, I can do that."

"I don't think that would be very honest. I'm not quite sure I know what to say either. I didn't imagine—no, that's not true."

"It's not?"

"Let's say," Vikram said, picking his words, "I had rather persuaded myself that what we did at school was just the usual boys' tomfoolery."

"Well, it was," Gil insisted, though he could still feel the memory of Vikram's lips on his, from five minutes and thirteen years ago.

"Yes, but I'm not a boy now. So..." Vikram let that trail off, as though he wasn't sure where 'so' would take him.

"Look, people have wants. And act on them, all the time, for all the law and the moralising that says not to, and what that tells me is we've all got our natures and there's no point making a fuss about it."

"I don't think it's quite that easy."

"Maybe not. But I reckon it's easier than being like that magistrate I told you about, pronouncing judgement from the Bench then sneaking in here with a muffler wrapped round his face because he's got an itch he can't let himself scratch. I see a lot of people who twist themselves up for wanting what they want, and damned if I know what good it does. And anyway—honestly, Vik, thirteen years? You'd've probably been able to fuck a rock by now if you found a pretty one."

Vikram stared at him and then began to laugh, at first looking startled by his own amusement and then uncontrollably, curling up on himself, so that Gil couldn't but laugh as well. "A rock? Did you say a *rock*?"

"A pretty one," Gil stressed. "Not any old rock."

"Talk about having a high opinion of yourself," Vikram spluttered.

"Whatever you say, rock-fucker."

Vikram howled at that, and Gil threw back his own head, feeling the momentary panic wash away in the mirth. Of course Vik could look after himself. He was a grown man, a clever one, nobody's fool and nobody's mark. He'd cope.

Everything was going to be fine.

Chapter Seven

If Vikram had been asked what his visit to Gilbert Lawless Bookseller would bring, he would not have imagined unlawful congress on the floor. He was just grateful the damned cat had been elsewhere.

The whole business probably ought to have felt terrifying or bewildering or shameful. It didn't. It had felt marvellous, frankly: the pure relief of his pent-up desires roaring free, the ecstatic thrill of physical sensation, the overwhelming closeness of kisses, so much more intimate than any other touch. It had been marvellous, and startlingly familiar, and *right*, as though he'd finally remembered something that had been nudging at his memory for years.

And wrong, too, because his lost friend ought not to be a scofflaw in this sordid trade, but under the hardened exterior he was still Gil. Still understanding, still funny, still unquenchable, or at least refusing to be quenched. Vikram had depended on Gil at school, always looking to him for the grin and the joke that would make things better, and he felt a tug of longing to have that once more. Someone who made him happy, whose purpose was to make life easier and pleasanter. As though he existed for Vikram's benefit. Vikram took people to court over that sort of thing all the time.

"Damnation," he said.

"What?"

"I think I just realised what a good friend to me you were, and how little I noticed."

Gil gave him an odd look. "What, because I tossed you off?"

"No, you fool. Because you made my life better in a dozen ways all the time. You're a great deal more caring than you pretend to be."

"I'm not." Gil sounded almost offended.

"Of course you are. At school–"

"That was a long time ago. Don't get ideas, mate, I wouldn't want to disappoint you."

There was a decidedly wary look in Gil's eyes. A moment ago he'd been so close, so tender and warm and careful and familiar, and Vikram was aware of a distinctly sinking sensation. He might not be experienced but he knew a put-off when he heard one, and that led his mind inexorably to a question he ought to have asked some time ago. "You aren't married, are you?"

Gil choked. "No."

"Why not?"

"Why should I be? You're not. I'm all right on my own."

"Are you happy? You asked me," Vikram added, at Gil's look.

"I'm fine. Doing all right."

"Not what I asked," Vikram said, mimicking Gil's tone from earlier, and got a glare for it.

"Don't come the lawyer with me, Sonny Jim. I'm looking after myself. I worked for that–a place of my own, money, stuff nobody can take away–and now I've got it. That's good enough for me."

Vikram wanted to argue that on about fifteen fronts at once, and felt himself entirely unqualified to do so. He nodded slowly, for lack of anything to say. They were still sprawled on the floor, the kind of position that had been perfectly comfortable in his youth and was now playing hob with his lower back. They ought to have been close, still kissing; he wanted painfully to be touching Gil, giving pleasure in return. But he'd managed to say the wrong damn thing, and he didn't have the least idea what the right thing would have been.

He wasn't given a chance to ask. Gil pushed himself up onto an elbow. "Come on, we've work to do. Let's finish looking through this lot."

What? No! "Right. Yes." Vikram tidied himself up as though this were quite normal, wondering if he'd missed an opportunity to do or say something he should have. Perhaps there hadn't been one. He had no idea what to do about Gil's tight, hard, defiant shell. He saw those often enough with his poorer clients, people so determined not to be hurt that they couldn't be helped.

Saw them and been no damned good at dealing with them, because it was an illogical and exasperating way to go on and he never knew how to act. He wished to hell he'd been reunited with Gil when Matthew Lawes was still alive. At the very least he could have rendered the vicious swine's last years a misery. Bloody Matthew, sitting on a hoard of degrading pictures like a dragon on a pile of gold.

Vikram flicked through his sordid collection, loathing the man more with every image, until his knees hurt from kneeling on the floor and he didn't think he'd ever expect to see anyone clothed again. He was just about to express his frustration when Gil said, "Hoi."

"What is it?"

"Got one."

Vikram scrambled over and looked at the photograph. "Yes, that's Sunil. And is that Errol with him, again?"

"That's him. There was a bunch in an opened envelope." Gil fanned out several pictures, all of them of the maximum-sentence-for-possession variety, and whistled. "These aren't pulling any punches. Different series to the other, isn't it?"

Vikram retrieved the first picture Gil had found of the two youths. "It's against a different background, certainly."

"The first one I found is earlier, I reckon. Sunil's got more of a moustache in the one you have there."

"Yes. And– Gil? Isn't this the same background as in the studio portrait? The one he gave his parents?"

He reached for the framed photograph as he spoke. Gil leaned over his shoulder, very close. Vikram could feel his warmth, his presence, as vividly as though they were both naked, skin to skin. "It might be, at that. Same pattern to the drapes, those pointy things. What do you call them?"

"Fleur-de-lys. More than that, though. Look at the way the pleats fall, the way it pools on the ground. These were surely taken at the same time." Vikram traced the line of the curtain, ignoring the boys in front of it.

"Same photographer, same session."

"And he gave the studio portrait to his parents a week before he disappeared."

Gil sat back on his heels. "That would be, what, the fourteenth of October or thereabouts?"

"Indeed. Why?"

"All right, look. Our snapper takes a set of pictures. A nice one of Sunil for Ma and Pa, then the clothes come off and he takes the rest. You'd develop them all in one go, wouldn't you?"

"I don't know anything about photography," Vikram admitted.

"I don't know much, but you get a lot of what they call negative images and you put them in trays of stuff to make prints, right? It's not a one-at-a-time job, is what I mean. If you go to a studio darkroom, there'll be a dozen pictures hanging up to dry."

"What are you getting at?"

"That it's likely all the pictures were developed at once," Gil said. "And I dare say a nice photograph would be a pretty special thing for a hard-up family—"

"It was a treasure. They kept it in a box. I had to swear to keep it safe before they'd let me take it."

"Exactly. So Sunil would surely want to bring his picture home for Ma and Pa right away. Maybe it might take a day or so for the print to dry, I don't know. But he wouldn't leave it lying around for a few weeks like it wasn't important, would he?"

Vikram thought of the Guptas' poor, shabby room. "No."

"Well. Say Sunil brought his picture home on the fourteenth, but Matthew had the dirty ones from the same session in his possession before he had his stroke on the twenty-first. That's a pretty quick turnaround to print them, offer them to him, get an agreement to buy, and send them to Wealdstone House by post."

Vikram tapped his fingers against his lips. "It is, isn't it. Would one send these things on approval?"

"Not without warning. You might send a letter to a collector saying you had new material and giving an idea what it might be, then he'd pay up and you'd send them. But for that to go back and forth in time, before he had the stroke..." Gil drummed his fingers on the floor. "Here's the thing. Have you seen anyone else of our colour in this lot?"

"Hardly any."

"Same. And scattered, yes? Individual images, not series. Whereas here you've got a whole set, and it's identical poses each way round. Errol sucks off Sunil, then vice versa, and same for the other positions."

Vikram wasn't sure where this was going, but didn't think he liked it. "What does that imply?"

"You must have noticed the albums are sorted by themes. Women together, people tied up, whips and stuff. Matthew liked things in sets. So we've got an album with pictures of the two lads doing one lot of things, and space left for more, and here are a lot of loose pictures of Errol and Sunil, filling in the gaps. In a manner of speaking."

"For goodness' sake."

"Sorry. Point is, I'm wondering if Matthew wanted a complete set. Of Errol and Sunil doing everything, or of a white boy with a brown one, or whatever it was in his head. But something like that."

Vikram assimilated that. "You think these new pictures were a commission? Posed for and taken on request."

"It's just a guess. And I don't know where it gets us, since he had his stroke before Errol died or Sunil left home. Still."

Vikram nodded slowly. "May I observe that your brother was disgusting?"

"No argument here."

"A rich man ordering people to commit acts as he might send out for a dish of meat—"

"Like dancing bears at the circus. I know."

Vikram wanted to spit. "Would the buyer have to pay extra for commissioned pictures?"

"Expect so."

"So there's money in it. And would Matthew have bought directly from the photographer?"

"Could be. If there was a middleman he'd need to be close. There wouldn't have been much time for back and forth."

"We need to find this photographer with the fleur-de-lys drapes," Vikram said with decision. "Somehow. How?"

Gil snorted. "You don't ask much. If there's any more pictures with the drapes in, I might recognise someone in them, I suppose. Or I could take them around to other people. There's a chap on Wych Street who knows everyone."

"Excellent. And... Do you know, I'm sure I saw those curtains earlier."

Gil looked around at the litter of photographs and piles of albums. "Seriously?"

"It's a noticeable pattern."

"Vik. Mate. When you look at dirty pictures, you're not meant to be thinking about the curtains."

"I thought you said people's pleasures are a matter of their nature, and their own business," Vikram said. "If I prefer curtains to postures, that is surely my affair."

"I'm going to get someone to do me a photographic series just for you. A rock in front of something nice, maybe in paisley. You'll be putty in my hands."

Vikram couldn't help but laugh, even if the jest flirted dangerously with his own wanting. "Just help me find the damned drapes, will you?"

Time ticked by. They had another cup of tea, and piled up a little heap: five images of depravity in front of fleur-de-lys curtains, all with people unknown to Gil. They had not mentioned their earlier encounter at all.

Vikram wanted to say something—*What did that mean? Did I do something wrong? Might we do it again?* He had no idea how to broach the subject, so he simply flicked through page after page, acres of meaningless two-dimensional flesh while Gil was three feet away, with his lean body, his warm mouth, his irresistible smile that set Vikram's pulse pounding every time.

Gil had said to come to him for a bit of fun, and hadn't suggested anything more. Vikram was not personally familiar with these situations, but he felt sure that one ought not ask for more than was on offer. If he wanted something other than what Gil could give, that was his own problem to resolve or, more truthfully, to bury under the heap of work where he put the other difficult questions.

It was hard not to imagine, or hope, that Gil had some of the answers to those. Vikram squashed that thought, and turned the page of an album with some force.

It brought him face to printed face with a woman well past her prime, cupping her breasts and pulling an expression of bliss so exaggerated as to look distinctly sarcastic, against a familiar background. "Curtains," Vikram said, adding the photograph to the pile.

Gil glanced over, then grabbed it with a yelp. "Yes! Finally."

"You know that woman?"

"Not in the Biblical sense; I like my prick not rotting away. But yes, I do. Her name's Annie Driver. We can drop in on her tomorrow, see if she remembers who took this thing."

"What? Why not now?"

"Because it's eight in the evening on a Saturday. She'll be busy, and I'm starving." He paused for a second. "In fact, I'm going to get a bite to eat now. Want to join me?"

Vikram did, except he couldn't quite forget Gil's face closing over earlier. Was this a politeness or a real invitation? Would it be asking too much? "I'm aware I've taken up most of your day. If you'd rather call it a night now—"

"It's up to you. Head off if you're busy."

That was doubtless a hint. He probably ought to go home; it would be only sensible. Vikram nodded, and rose.

Gil stood too, looking as though he were about to speak, stopped himself, then put a hand out, just brushing Vikram's forearm. Such a light touch, barely perceptible through his sleeve, but Vikram couldn't help a little shiver at the contact. "If you're not busy, though, I wouldn't mind catching up properly, without all this gubbins in our way. And they do a good bill of fare at the Coal Hole."

Vikram felt a wave of relief. This was absolutely an invitation, if only to a meal, but really, a meal with an old friend was a sufficiently pleasant prospect and there was no need to read anything warmer than that into Gil's words. "Well. Yes, all right. A bite to eat. Why not?"

The next morning Vikram was awake at six. He usually woke early; on this occasion he'd been disturbed by the chime of unfamiliar bells. St. Clement's church was very close to Holywell Street.

Next to him, Gil snored softly, his hair a tangled cloud tickling Vikram's skin.

The previous evening was, for the most part, a mass of sensation in his memory. That first encounter, the disturbing effect of those accursed photographs, the desire in Gil's eyes. He'd wanted so much—Gil's longing, his pleasure, his touch—and in the wildness of the moment he'd let himself have it.

And he'd kept wanting even as they'd gone to dinner, Gil leading him through some stinking little passageway onto the Strand and down to the Coal Hole public house. They'd eaten a surprisingly good meal there, talking of old times, old acquaintance, and then anything. Music for example: Gil liked music hall; Vikram liked the opera. Or politics: Vikram had voted Liberal after the passing of the Reform Act; Gil hadn't bothered. Or books: Gil loved the old Gothic romances, and waxed lyrical about Mrs Radcliffe, William Beckford, and Mrs Swann; Vikram hadn't read a novel in years.

In fact, they hadn't agreed on a single thing, except that Vikram would come back to the bookshop afterwards. To have a proper chat about what had to be done, Gil had said. But he'd grabbed Vikram's hand as they went up the wooden stairs, ale on his breath and light in his eyes, and tugged him to a different door, and Vikram had followed, that old, glorious sensation of adventure mingling with an entirely new set of hope and yearning and desire.

And here he was now at six in the morning, with Gil lying naked next to him in a dingy bedroom above a pornographic bookshop.

They hadn't done...well, many of the things he'd seen in the photographs. Just body to body, kissing and rubbing and hands. Vikram suspected it had been unsophisticated stuff, but Gil had seemed entirely content. He'd laughed, and made Vikram laugh, and voiced his pleasures openly in a way that had turned the evening into something not just ecstatic, but easy.

That was what Vikram couldn't quite grasp, a thing too big to reach. Gil did these things as if they were—damn the word—fun. Not important, not earthshaking, not the first time Vikram had trusted another adult with his body and skin and the truth of his desires, and his hopeless, helpless yearning for something outside the life he'd so painstakingly built around himself. Simply a thing that felt good.

Vikram would not have called it disappointing, far from it. He'd reached the peak of pleasure twice last night, consumed with the bliss of shared sensation, hopelessly responsive to Gil's touch. Gil had straddled him the second time, wrapping both their members in his work-hardened hand. The feel of that, of them pressing together—Vikram had to shut his eyes in the darkness because the memory was having an effect now. Still, afterwards, with Gil lying in the crook of his arm, a small part of him had undeniably felt rather flat that something so long denied had turned out to be so very simple.

Which was an irony, because now, with noise starting to rise from the Strand even this early on a Sunday morning, and his vivid awareness that he was naked in Gil's bed, this suddenly didn't seem simple at all. What the devil had he done?

Well, he'd committed multiple acts of gross indecency, breaking the law for the first time in his adult life. He felt absolutely no remorse, let alone guilt, about that, nor did he find himself particularly afraid of legal consequences, since he was quite sure Gil knew what he was about. In fact, and somewhat to his own surprise, all of his many worries were focused on what might happen when Gil woke up.

With any other man—if this had been conceivable with any other man—he might have feared to see shame, disgust, remorse on the face next to his. He didn't fear those with Gil, but he was still undeniably afraid, and that fact was frightening all by itself.

He was afraid that Gil would wake up and shrug and go about his business. He was terrified of seeing indifference or, worse, the desire to get away. He still had no idea what Gil wanted of him, if it was anything approaching the hunger Vikram felt for his company, his intimacy. He didn't know how one was meant to conduct oneself in this situation, or what was reasonable to expect, still less want. And as for the possibility that Gil might consider last night no more than a pleasant evening's diversion–

"Christ," Gil mumbled into the pillow. "You all right?"

Vikram could just make out that Gil had one bleary eye open, his face smeared into the bolster. He looked down, not knowing what to say.

"Only you're stiff as a sergeant. And not in a good way." Gil hoisted himself up onto an elbow and gave a sleepy grin. "I knew you'd be a morning sort. Don't tell me, you're always at work by eight."

"Half past seven, usually."

"God. What time is it?"

"Just gone six."

"*God.* That's why they say virtue is its own reward. I prefer the wages of sin."

"Idle hound. Can we visit your lady today?"

"She's no lady, and she's not going to be up for a while yet." Gil sat up, reaching for matches, and lit the candle by his bed. It flared into guttering life with a stink of tallow. He narrowed his eyes against the light, then reached out to run a finger over Vikram's eyebrow. "God's truth, you can frown. You could win medals for it."

"It's a useful professional skill."

"I bet. Are you all right?"

"Of course."

"Is that 'of course' meaning 'leave me alone, that never happened', or 'of course, that was the best night of my life, fancy sucking my cock?'"

Vikram couldn't manage an answer. Gil's brow slanted. "Right. I'm guessing the first."

"No. Or—well— Neither. Don't put words in my mouth."

"Put some there yourself, then, because it would help if I knew what you were thinking."

"That makes two of us," Vikram said. "This isn't precisely within my experience."

"I know. I suppose it's not much use asking what you want, either?"

"I refer the court to my previous answer."

Gil grinned, but there was a frown between his brows. "Look, mate. We had a good time last night, right?"

"Yes. Yes, we did. Or at least, I did."

"And I did too, and that makes *we*. Well, if you want more, I'm right here. If you don't, that's fair enough; just say so. I won't make a fuss. And if you're worried about doing harm, or getting caught, you won't hurt me, and I won't blab. So it's up to you, whatever you want. All right?"

Vikram blinked. "It must be more complicated than that."

"Why? We can fuck if you like and not if you don't want to. What's complicated?"

"What about what *you* want?"

Gil gave him a long, slow look. It was deliberate, up and down, taking his time. His eyes were brown-gold, like a glass of ale raised to the light, and the expression in them brought the blood up in Vikram's cheeks. "Like I say. If you want more, I'm right here."

Apparently that was as close as he'd come to asking for more. Was he unwilling to say the words, or simply not greatly concerned either way? "Why?" Vikram blurted.

"Why what?"

Why all of it. Why had he done this, why was it Gil, why had it always been Gil, why had he been gone for thirteen damned years, and why couldn't Vikram find the right words to say what he meant, or ask what he needed? "Well, why me?" he asked, as somewhere to begin.

"What? Mate," Gil said. "You need to ask?"

It sounded like that meant Vikram oughtn't. He said, "Yes," all the same, because he didn't have much time for questions that shouldn't be asked.

Gil's brow furrowed. "All right, if you must know. Because, these." His finger traced Vikram's thick brows. "I always liked your eyebrows. Because of these." The fingertip slid down, circling Vikram's eye socket. "Bloody great beak of a nose, scowl like a pissed-off god, and eyes like a puppy-dog. Because..." He contemplated Vikram with an almost puzzled look. "Because I can feel your heart thumping from here. Because the way you looked when I brought you off yesterday was so exactly like my best mate. Because I'm glad you haven't changed. Because I missed you."

"I missed you too," Vikram whispered.

Gil was watching his eyes, looking almost uncertain, which wasn't right. "Yeah. Only— "

"What?"

"Ah, Vik. *I've* changed, even if you haven't. I've a pretty shabby life here and I know it. It's mine, and nobody's taking it off me, which is something. But there you are, fighting the world, and here I am, selling dirty books."

"Here you are," Vikram agreed. "Surviving and thriving, swimming when other people would have sunk. I'm glad of everything you did, so long as it kept you alive. And I don't think you have changed so much. You still make me laugh, and your eyes laugh when you do it. You still pretend you don't care when you do."

"I do not."

"Which is why you spent all yesterday helping me look for a needle in a haystack."

"Don't call them needles where the boys can hear."

Vikram gave him a rebuking look. "You said, whatever I want, yes?"

"Within reason," Gil said cautiously.

"Very well. I want you not to vanish out of my life again, however that is best achieved. And I want you to tell me if I'm falling short of the, uh, the correct standards of behaviour in these matters, because I'm damned if I know what I'm doing."

"This is Holywell Street. You can't fall when you're already on the floor."

"You know what I mean. I've no idea of how one goes about negotiating intimacies."

"You hurt my head," Gil said. "Negotiating– Jesus. You *ask*, Vik. Preferably in human words. Say what you'd like, ask what I'd like, tell me if something isn't right for you, and listen to what I say. That's all. You're not going to come up with anything I haven't heard before."

"But one can't simply say, 'Fancy sucking'—you know."

"One bloody can, in the right company. And yes, since you ask, I do." Gil gave him an evil grin. "*If* you can get the words out.

I'm not 'embarking on negotiations pertaining to fellatio' or whatever, so don't even try."

"Proper terminology is important," Vikram said. "I may have to work up to it."

They were both lying on their sides, faces close. He leaned in, and saw Gil's lips curve as he mirrored the movement. Their mouths met, lazy and sticky with sleep, and Vikram let himself sink into the sensation as Gil's hand slid over his hip. He reached out, angling his arm awkwardly to get his hand to Gil's sinewy back, pulling him close.

It could have been years ago, this silent touching. And then again it couldn't, and that wasn't down to the rasp of beard against skin, the broader bodies and heavier muscles. It was that once upon a time the world had been full of possibility and excitement and wonder, and now it held difficulty and years of toil to come, and defeat after inevitable defeat. And yet here they were, Vikram and Gil, once again making themselves a space in which they could, perhaps, be happy.

He leaned in harder. Gil gave a startled but appreciative grunt in his mouth, and then they were both moving with urgency, flesh and muscle hard against one another, pushing for warmth and closeness in the chilly air.

And what the hell. He might not have done this for thirteen years, but he'd seen every conceivable permutation of intimacy over the last day, which had undeniably refreshed his memory. He pulled his mouth from Gil's with a gasp. "You mentioned negotiations pertaining to fellatio?"

"Jesus *Christ*," Gil muttered, then made a startled noise as Vikram crawled down the bed over him, trailing his tongue against the lean planes of his belly. Gil clearly did a lot of heavy lifting. "You're making a good case so far. Ah, fuck, yes."

Getting into place required a certain amount of manoeuvring. Vikram was nearly six feet, the bed wasn't huge and had an iron rail at the end, the room was freezing if he wasn't under blankets and the air restricted if he was. But Gil shunted up and pulled the covers around, and Vikram got there.

The memories came back with vivid clarity once Gil was in his mouth: the feel of firm flesh, the ridges and contours, the slight musky taste, the tickle of hair against his face, most of all, the effect it had. Gil's hands in his hair, his sotto voce murmurs of pleasure. Vikram explored with increasing confidence, remembering little discoveries: to hollow one's cheeks for suction, to slide the lips up and down the full length, to run one's tongue around the smooth head and then take the whole length back down.

"Christ," Gil said. "Vik."

Vikram slid fingers around Gil's shaft, working him, relishing the sense of control. He could feel the tension in his body, the taut muscles of his thighs, the odd astringent tang in his mouth that told him Gil was close. All of it so wonderfully familiar, as though they'd barely been interrupted, as though the divided years had been nothing more than a rock in the riverbed around which the waters flowed and rejoined.

"Mate," Gil rasped. "So good. Bit faster? Christ, Vik. *Jesus.* Going to come, shift your arse."

Vikram pulled off hastily, if reluctantly. He'd let Gil spend in his mouth before, but in those days he hadn't cared where he spat. He kept up the movement of his fingers, though, stroking, licking, urging Gil on and feeling his own arousal grow in tandem, until he heard that familiar hiccup of breath, and felt Gil convulse under his hand as he spent, the spunk splashing pale against his belly. "Ah, Christ, yes, *yes.* Yes. God, that was good."

Vikram released him, feeling decidedly self-satisfied, and rather more secure in his own competence. He fought his way back up the bed, attempting not to dislodge the blankets too badly, and ended up with his head pillowed on Gil's shoulder and slung arm over his chest, inevitably failing to avoid the cooling sticky mess. He didn't even care.

"Am I squashing you?" he thought to ask.

"Don't flatter yourself, you're not that big." Gil exhaled, long and satisfied. "God, Vik. I'd completely forgotten you were good at that."

Forgotten, Vikram thought, feeling the cold draft of reality slice through the warmth. Well, of course Gil had forgotten. He'd had plenty of experience since their schooldays, after all, and doubtless it all merged into one after a while for people who had earned other memories rather than living in limbo. Vikram had no right to demand to be remembered, and no reason to expect Gil to do so, or to colour *now* with memories of *then*. He would do well to keep that in mind.

Chapter Eight

They went off to find Annie Driver around ten. It was a Sunday and she'd have been up late into the night; there was no point rushing. Plus, that allowed them a leisurely Sunday morning in bed together, and Gil had enjoyed that to the full. He'd returned the favour Vik had done him, showing him a few extra tricks he'd picked up along the way, and could have spent again himself just watching the way Vikram responded to him. The gasping abandon, the trust, the way his brows angled into a ferocious frown when he came.

It had been good. It had been bloody good, and not just because Vik had grown up mouthwatering, either. It had been...special.

Gil hadn't trusted anyone for a long time. He could pretty much put an exact date on the last day he'd done that, in fact; he still felt the agonising wound of his father's betrayal even though he knew now Matthew's words had been a lie. He'd believed the hurt too long to forget it, and remembered too many other, smaller wounds his father had inflicted without even noticing. *Pity you take after your mother, boy.* Passing remarks, little disparagements, papercuts in his self-esteem but they'd mounted up over the years, and made it possible for him to believe the great lie.

He hadn't trusted anyone since then, as well he shouldn't in this shitty line of work. He also hadn't had a conversation of the old kind—the ones about literature and politics and such—since William Dugdale had gone down for the last time. Dugdale been a bright man, well educated, with a lot to say about principles and the philosophy of free speech. That fatal stint in Clerkenwell had been his fifth trip to gaol; he'd gone into a decline and died behind bars, a sorry mumbling shadow of himself. Gil didn't want to end up like that.

And here was Vikram, reminding him that he'd had a different life once and a different future. Not reducing him to his line of work, but talking like Gil was his equal still. It felt as though they were still the friends they had been, as though he could count on Vik when he needed help. That meant something, because it was exhausting to always be at loggerheads with the world, and Vik knew that as well as Gil did. It would be...pretty good, really, to have someone on your side.

Gil hadn't had that in years because people were bastards, because they lied and cheated and let you down and forgot and didn't care. But if there was a soul alive he would turn to in trouble, he had an absurd feeling it would be Vik, and that was frightening in its implications. Vikram had expectations, and standards, and he wouldn't give them up for the sake of a fuck. Not that Gil would want him to, naturally, but that brought problems of its own.

Because, as they paced along eastwards up Fleet Street towards the Golden Lane rookery, through the thick, grimy air, Gil felt...not quite right, and he wasn't sure why. Like he'd said something he shouldn't have, or missed saying something he should.

He'd come bloody near to blurting things that he had no right to ask at all. He might want Vik to stick around, but to say so would be unfair as well as stupid. Vik had an overactive sense of responsibility, and Gil had seen the angry pity in his eyes, as well as the need. If Gil asked him for more time together, he'd probably get it, and tangle them both up in his own sordid mess, and Vik was a lawyer with a good name to lose. He had to look after himself.

Anyway, Gil didn't want anyone's pity, or need anyone's help, and he had a living to make. Any stupid thoughts he might have about staying Vikram's one and only needed to be filed away with the rest of the dreams that he didn't have time to mourn. They'd found each other and enjoyed each other for the night. They'd had fun. Why couldn't that be enough? Where was the sense in letting one night start you thinking about more nights, all the nights, forever?

The circling thoughts carried him all the way to Long Lane in silence which Vikram didn't break. Evidently he also had things on his mind.

Gil popped into the Old Red Cow to confirm Annie's direction with a mate there, and shot Vikram a quick look as he emerged, him in his smart greatcoat and shiny shoes. "Do you want to wait here for me?"

"Why should I not come with you?"

"Golden Lane. It's a bit rough."

"Shad Thames is hardly pleasant," Vikram said. "And I am not a shrinking violet."

"Well, they're your shoes, you can ruin them if you like."

Vikram merely snorted. He did, nevertheless, slow down somewhat as they proceeded, picking his way through puddles and runnels of filth. Golden Lane was a stinking maze of human ordure, with the odd chicken in the street, half-clothed children and half-starved cats. A few bits of damp washing flapped above their heads, already streaked with grime from the foul air. It was a typical enough rookery; Gil wished he'd brought a blackjack.

They were attracting attention as well. It wasn't a part of the world where many Indians congregated, and you didn't get a lot of people of any sort dressed like Vikram. He looked like a do-gooder, or the law, and nobody here was in the market for either. Gil caught the eye of a brat picking up a handful of slime to throw, and gave her a warning headshake. He applauded the sentiment, but she could pick on some other toff.

Annie lived down a nameless alley in lodgings. Gil knocked on the door till an unshaven, shirtsleeved man answered, talked them in, and within no more than fifteen minutes a yawning Annie Driver came into the tiny kitchen, wearing only a nightgown and flannel robe. He could feel Vikram's shock.

Annie was a good laugh, an older woman who'd been round and about for years, had her share of knocks, drank more than her share of gin. It was a shitty life, Gil had no doubt, but she made the best fist she could of it, grinning her gap-toothed grin.

"All right, Annie," he said. "Sorry to wake you."

"All right, Gil. Who's the tall dark stranger?"

"Mate of mine. He's got a few questions."

She gave him a skewed look. "You bringing the law to my door?"

"Wouldn't dream of it. We just need help picking out curtains."

That set Annie roaring. She threw her head back, wheezily cackling till the tears came, and Gil laughed with her until she calmed down. "Go on then, what is it?"

Gil brought out the picture of her. He'd made sure he carried the photographs in case of trouble; he didn't want Vikram caught with those on him. "This bit of art, love."

"That's me, young and beautiful." She waggled her bosom in Vikram's direction and cackled again.

"Pick on someone your own size," Gil told her. "Do you remember who took this one?"

"The photographer?" Annie blinked. "Why'd you want to know that?"

"Nothing that'll be trouble for you. We just need to track him down." She glanced at Vikram, clearly unconvinced. Gil wished the bugger had stayed in the pub. "It's not about your picture, Annie, I promise. Ah, look." He fished out one of the Errol and Sunil pictures. "It's about this. Looks like it was taken in the same—"

"That's Errol," she said.

"Yeah."

"Errol that got his head beat in. I don't know anything about this. What's going on?"

"Now, calm down," Gil said soothingly.

"We don't know," Vikram put in, his deep voice authoritative. "It may well be nothing. But you will not be asked to come forward, and your name will not be committed to paper of any sort, nor will it be revealed to the photographer, nor will any photograph or image of you be passed to the authorities. You have my word that you will hear no more of this."

Annie's brows rose, but evidently Vikram's manner had a magic of its own, because she leaned forward and said, quickly, "Thomas Oswald, on Great Wild Street. And I didn't tell you that if there's any trouble."

"Madam, I have never met you in my life," Vikram assured her so gravely that he won a reluctant grin. "And—speaking as someone you have never met and never will—do you happen to recognise the other one?"

She squinted at the picture, then up at Vikram. "Friend of yours? Son?"

"No. Just a boy."

"I don't know him. Of course I don't mix with the young'uns so much these days, but..." She shook her head. "New to the game, was he?"

"Was?" Vikram asked.

Annie gave him a very old look. "*Is* turns to *was* quick enough on the streets, sir. Look at poor Errol, God rest him."

Vikram nodded. "Thank you for your help."

They made their goodbyes and headed back to civilisation, or at least to slightly cleaner streets, which was almost the same thing. "You handled her well," Gil said as they picked their way out of the twisting lanes.

"I have done this kind of thing before, you know."

"I suppose." Gil didn't really know why he'd assumed Vikram couldn't talk to reluctant witnesses, except that this was his world. He'd expected, maybe wanted, to be Vikram's guide. "She's a good woman, Annie. Hard life. Buried five children. What did you give her?"

"Two ten-shilling notes," Vikram said. "I suppose she'll spend it on gin."

"Probably. I would if I was her."

"Did you recognise the name she gave?"

"Can't say I did. Shall we go there now? It's convenient for home, and we're already cold and wet." Great Wild Street was roughly between Holywell Street and Lincoln's Inn. Gil wondered which 'home' Vikram would have thought he meant. "If he's not open we can come back Monday. Which... Do you think you'd better stay outside on this one, Vik? It's one thing talking to Annie—she's spent plenty of time in the cells for disorderly, and she doesn't have much to lose. But taking and selling the pictures of the boys is a different matter. This fellow isn't going to admit anything to the law by choice. I wouldn't in his shoes."

"No. Do you think he'll talk to you?"

Gil nodded. "He'll know of me, for certain: I'm the only bookseller of colour on Holywell Street. I reckon he's more likely to talk to me on my own."

"You're probably right."

"Anything particular you want me to ask? What are you hoping he'll tell you?"

Vikram shrugged. "Anything at all. Presumably he must have made conversation with his subjects, ah, in between. He might know the name of Sunil's gentleman friend, or have some clue in that direction, or know if Sunil had any intention to go anywhere. He could confirm if your half-brother or someone else ordered the pictures. I don't know, Gil, I'm clutching at straws. I just want something I can tell Sunil's parents."

"I can't promise that," Gil said drily. "But you never know. I'll do what I can."

He'd wondered if they'd have trouble finding this Thomas Oswald on Great Wild Street. In fact the man had a sign advertising photographic services on the door of a nondescript and dusty insurance office.

"I suppose he works out the back," Gil said, as they stood in front of the door. The shop was shuttered; upstairs the curtains were closed. "Tell you what, you get a couple of mugs of tea from the stall we passed while I see if anyone's in. If he is, you'll need them both to warm up while you wait, and if he isn't, I'm dying for a cuppa."

"You could have one first," Vikram suggested. "You've taken a great deal of time to help me with this. You needn't deny yourself tea."

"It hasn't been a hardship."

"Maybe not. But you dropped everything to help me, and trudged around in this vile weather, and I felt you should know I don't take it for granted. I appreciate that you did that for me."

There was just the slightest hesitation before the last two words, and he wore what Gil knew to be a slight frown, though anyone else would have seen an intimidating scowl. Christ, Gil loved his eyebrows. Christ, he wanted Vik around.

For me. Was that a question, and how the hell was he supposed to answer it?

"Anything for you, sweetheart," he said, and instantly regretted the sarcastic tone, but had no idea how to remedy it. "You get your tea. I'll knock this Oswald up."

Vikram nodded, turned and trudged off through the crusty street sludge. Gil looked after him for a moment, increasingly sure he'd buggered that up. But what could he say? *Of course I'd do this for you. I'd do pretty much anything that kept you around for a while. Except I wouldn't, because I know you shouldn't stay.*

Vikram deserved better. Someone as upstanding as himself, without an ugly past and gnarly scars, a partner who'd aid in his work and not be an embarrassment to a decent lawyer. And as such, it was stupid for Gil to feel he'd done wrong by not saying anything. He wouldn't have done either of them any good.

Whereas he could do this now so he ought to get on with it. He rapped on the door, then stepped back and looked up, catching just a twitch of movement at the curtain. He waited a few minutes, then knocked again. On the third round, the door opened.

"Yes?"

"I'm looking for Thomas Oswald."

The man at the door was thin-faced, sallow-white, his last shave a few days ago. He stretched his lips out in a perfunctory extension that sufficed for a smile. "You have him. Can I help you?"

"Could you spare me a quarter hour?" Gil asked. "My name's Gil Lawless–"

"Sittings by appointment only and not on a Sunday."

"It's not a sitting. I've a few questions."

"I don't work on Sunday. You'll need to come back tomorrow."

"Professional query, mate," Gil said. "I'm in your line of work. Gilbert Lawless, bookseller, on Holywell Street."

Oswald's face went blank. Gil knew the expression well; he used it himself. "I don't know what you mean."

"I'm not here to make trouble."

"You can come back on Monday."

"I'm here now," Gil said. "Fifteen minutes and I'll be out of your hair."

"Well, maybe you can–"

Oswald shut the door on those words, and looked quite startled when it failed to close because Gil's foot was in the way.

"Seeing as I'm here, professional query," Gil said, smiling nicely. "Fifteen minutes of your time, plus as long as you want to stand here letting the cold in."

Oswald had a sort of blank, heavy look to his face. "You might as well come in and explain."

He led the way to the back room, which had a skylight for all the good it did in this miserable weather, and was full of photographic clutter, tables, boxes of props and the like. Several sets of drapes hung on a free-standing screen, including a shabby blue length with a familiar fleur-de-lys pattern. It was cold, and Gil couldn't see a stove.

"Do you have a fire when you're taking your pictures?" he asked. "I'd have thought it gets chilly with no clothes on."

"Who are you?" Oswald demanded. "What do you want?"

"Gil Lawless, Holywell Street, like I said." He was starting to wonder if the bloke had been drinking, and if so what. He wouldn't rule out laudanum. "I need to ask you about some lads you photographed."

"Are you with the police?"

Fuck's sake. "I'm a bookseller. Books and prints. You make the stuff, I sell it. We're in the same line, savvy?"

"Who are you working with? Why are you here?"

"For crying out loud." Gil was rapidly running out of patience. "Listen, will you? You"—he pointed at Oswald's face to aid understanding—"took some pictures of a boy I know, all right? Pictures with him and another lad together. I'm trying to find out what happened to him *after* you took those pictures. Where he went, who he went to see, anything like that."

"Why are you asking me?"

"Because this is the last place he was seen," Gil said, overstating the matter somewhat in the effort to get through the fog in Oswald's mind. "We've followed his trail, it's got us here. I want you to tell me where to look next. Understand?"

"Who says I know anything?" Oswald asked. "What do you mean, trail?"

Gil fished out the photograph of Sunil and Errol, and handed it to Oswald. “That was taken in this room, wasn’t it? That’s the curtain over there.”

Oswald didn’t bother to look round. He was staring at the picture.

“When did you take it?” Gil pressed.

“I don’t know. A few weeks ago.”

“Was it done to commission?”

The colour went from Oswald’s cheeks. “Why, wh-why are you asking? Why does it matter?”

“Because there’s people want to know what happened to him. Shall we stop messing about? The quicker you tell me everything you know, the quicker we can sort it out.”

Oswald looked up from the picture at last. “Yes. Of course. I, uh—I can tell you something. It was a commission, yes, but I can’t reveal the name of the client, you understand, that would be—” His eyes flickered, as though he was looking for policemen in the shadows.

“Matthew Lawes of Wealdstone House,” Gil said, not making it a question.

Oswald’s eyes widened sharply, and he swallowed before speaking. “You— How— Yes. Yes, that’s right. I suppose you want to know about that.”

By God he did. “Yes.”

“Here. Sit down.” Oswald shoved a wooden chair in his direction. Its legs scraped on the floor. “I have a letter, from Mr. Lawes, let me find it. It will explain everything. You’ll see.”

Gil’s skin prickled. *Explain.* If his shitbag brother had played a part in Sunil’s disappearance—he didn’t know what he’d do but he’d tear the family apart rather than let that be covered up. He took the seat, thinking hard.

Oswald was still ferreting in a pile of papers. He said, “Sorry, I must have put it...” in a feeble sort of way and went to search on a shelf behind Gil.

Suppose Sunil had gone to Wealdstone House, Gil thought. Suppose the pictures weren’t enough, and Matthew had wanted him in person. Suppose he’d arrived to find Matthew lying unconscious, drifting out of life, and Matthew’s lackey Vilney—or even Horace?—had decided to shut the boy up. The thought brought up goosebumps, the thrill of discovery along with a growing, angry urge to avenge whatever had been done to the boy, and he twisted impatiently to ask Oswald where this damned letter was.

That meant he saw the photographer in the act of swinging a mallet down at his skull.

Gil hurled himself sideways off the chair. The savage blow landed on his shoulder as he went down, and rebounded to connect with the side of his head, and he found himself sprawled on the hard, dusty floor, unable to understand anything but blinding pain. He heard a vague sound, as though Oswald was speaking through water, and tried to force himself up but his left arm didn’t seem to be working. He shoved as hard as he could with his right, pushing himself feebly along, and the mallet came down again with floorboard-splintering force about four inches from his face.

Gil’s ears were clearing slightly, although the pain was building in proportion. He heard Oswald gave an angry sob.

“Just stay still! Just stop it! I don’t want to do this!”

“Fucking don’t, then!” Gil’s tongue felt thick. He scrabbled backwards, shoulder and head throbbing in a very bad way, a nasty wet feeling on his face. Oswald’s face was a mask of horror and misery even as he raised the mallet again. “Stop it!”

"I didn't ask you to come!" Oswald shouted. "I don't want to do it! This is your fault! It was his fault, and now it's your fault!"

Gil had his back to the wall now, shoulders propped up, but he couldn't seem to stand and he needed to. If he stayed on the floor, even this lunatic couldn't keep on missing his shots, and that mallet wouldn't have to land twice to crush his skull.

Just as Errol's skull had been crushed, and his body dumped in Clare Court, only a few streets from here.

Shit.

"You killed Errol," he said, staring up at the man and the mallet.

"It wasn't my fault!" Oswald sounded actually defensive, standing over Gil on the floor. "He *made* me do it, it wasn't my fault, and why do you care anyway? Why would anyone care? But now you're here and I'm going to have to– Oh God! Why couldn't you just leave me alone?"

"But I'm not here about Errol," Gil said blankly. "I was looking for Sunil."

"Who?"

"The other one!"

Oswald's mouth dropped open. He stared at the mallet in his hand as though he wasn't sure what to do with it. Gil had a wild second's hope they might be able to chalk this up to a misunderstanding, no harm done, and then Oswald looked at him again, his face hardening.

"I'm very sorry about that," he said. "But it's too late. It's all too late. I don't have a choice any more."

He raised the mallet, and took a step closer, and in the passage a deep voice called, "Is anyone there?"

"Vik!" Gil screamed at the top of his lungs. "*Help!*"

Oswald turned fast, and Gil yelled, "Watch out!" as Vikram came slamming into the room, because if he'd brought Vikram into danger— He tried and failed to push himself up as Oswald charged forward, bringing the mallet in a wild sideways sweep that missed by a foot. Vikram recoiled, cast one wide-eyed glance at Gil, and tossed the contents of the steaming mug he held into Oswald's face.

The photographer screamed. He didn't drop the mallet, but he swiped at his eyes with his free hand, and Vikram barrelled in before he could gather his wits, pushing close to stop Oswald getting another swing in. It was done with some power, because Vikram was big, but what the fuck was a lawyer going to do against a lunatic—

Vikram brought his knee up. There was an audible impact of flesh and bone, and Oswald bent in two, folding to the floor with a strangled, high-pitched noise.

Vikram stooped and grabbed the mallet. He looked at it, looked at Gil over the other side of the room, and returned his gaze to Oswald with an expression so purely murderous Gil thought for a moment he might lift the thing and bring it down.

"Oi," he rasped.

Vikram swung round, tossing the mallet to one side. "Gil. What happened?"

"He killed Errol. Hit me on the head."

Vikram hurried over to kneel by him. "You're bleeding. Where are you injured? Can you see me? Are you all right? How many fingers am I holding up? Gil!"

"Jesus, calm down," Gil muttered unfairly, because what he actually wanted was for Vikram to hold him and not let go. "Fine. 'S just a knock."

Vikram's hand hovered over the side of his head. "This looks bad. Don't move. I'll get a doctor."

"No!" The idea of Vikram going off and leaving him with Oswald was very, very bad. "Stay. Please."

Vikram cupped his face. His hand felt rather hot, unless Gil felt excessively cold, and his eyes were intent. "I won't leave you, I promise. And you may not leave me. All this blood—ah, the devil." He shut his eyes.

I thought I was dead till you turned up. He could have killed me, and I'd have left you standing in the street with some stupid put-off remark as the last thing I said to you.

Gil couldn't get that out, but he managed to lift his good hand to cover Vikram's, needing the touch. "I'm fine. Nothing broken." He hoped not, at least. His shoulder hurt, and he really didn't want to be sick on Vikram.

"Keep still," Vikram told him. "Listen. I do need to find someone, get them to send for a doctor and the police. I swear I won't be long."

"Oswald," Gil managed. "If he gets up..."

"I know. Just a minute." Vikram looked around the room in a vague sort of way as he rose, then gave a little nod to himself. He walked over to Oswald, who was still on the floor, screwed up his face, and, to Gil's pure astonishment, kicked the man in the balls with the kind of force that suggested he'd been winning pub fights all his life.

Oswald made a noise like deflating india-rubber and curled up. Gil couldn't blame him. "Jesus, Vik!"

"Well, it'll keep him occupied," Vikram said apologetically. He grabbed the mallet. "And I'll take this with me. Hold on."

He darted out, leaving Gil alone with Oswald's airless whimpers, and a new respect for Vikram's problem-solving powers.

It only took a few minutes for him to return, at a run. "Help's on its way. All right?"

Gil tried a smile he didn't feel. "Fine."

"Good. I raised the alarm and sent a boy to find a policeman. They'll be here soon. Meanwhile..." Vikram strode over to the whimpering photographer, reached down and hauled him up by his shirt front. Oswald made no effort at resistance. "Right. You will give me some answers. I would advise you not to try my patience."

Oswald started bleating. Gil couldn't listen. He rested his throbbing head against the wall and thought dizzily about Sunil, and Errol, and Vikram's mission, and Oswald's words. *Why would anyone care?*

"Hello? What's going on here?"

It was a deep unfamiliar voice. Gil looked up and saw the blue serge of a police uniform, and his heart stopped.

Police. Fuck. With Vik here in this studio, the photographic evidence to hand—he knew how this went, they'd arrest everyone around and the magistrates had no mercy. He and Vik might even end up in Pentonville, like that other poor bastard, and there was no way Vikram would survive not talking for two months, it would kill him. Gil sat, frozen in an icy sea of panic, as Vikram spoke to the constable. He wanted to scream at the stupid sod to run, and had to bite his lips on the inside to keep silent.

The big policeman clomped over, heavy boots thudding on the floorboards. "Are you Mr. Lawless, sir?"

"He is," Vikram said. "And as you can see, he is injured, and in no condition to answer questions that will inevitably be repeated by your superiors. Now, may I suggest–"

Gil let the flow of words wash over him, until, to his vague surprise, the constable disappeared. He had no idea how Vik had swung that, but he couldn't miss the opportunity it gave. "Mate?" he rasped.

Vikram came over, brows drawing together, and knelt by him. "What is it?"

"We'll have to tell them about the pictures, to see this bastard hang." Gil's head was none too clear but he was sure of that much. "You don't want to be involved. Get out before they get here, the rest of the peelers, I mean. Clear off. I'll do it."

Vikram blinked. "Are you all right?"

"Go." Gil wasn't even entirely sure if that would be possible, now Vikram had talked to the coppers like a fool, but they'd just have to try. He could take a stretch better than Vik could. "I can handle this."

"What do you mean, handle it? You can't even focus."

Gil gripped his hand. "They'll arrest you. Not having that. Get *out*."

"For heaven's sake," Vikram said, sounding half way between exasperated and choked. "I am searching for Sunil at the request of his parents."

"No real names," Gil insisted. "I'll make something up. George Smith, I dunno. Just *go*, will you?"

"Gil." Vikram's hold on his hand was so tight, so warm. "You've had a bang on the head. I am not in your trade, remember? I'm a lawyer. I promise you I won't suffer for my involvement in the slightest, and I'm damned if you will either. I won't let you go to gaol for anything and certainly not for me, you ridiculous– Do you understand? I'm in charge here. It's *all right.*"

Gil blinked muzzily, but Vikram sounded so certain that it was hard to argue. Maybe he knew something Gil didn't. "Is it?"

"I promise. Do you trust me?"

"Course."

Vikram tugged his hand up and Gil felt the lightest brush of lips over his fingers. "Then be quiet. Er, do you mind if your family is brought into it?"

"Fuck 'em."

"I didn't think so." Vikram smiled blurrily, unless that was Gil's vision, and squeezed his fingers. "Please try not to fret, and sit quietly while we wait for the doctor. In fact, stop talking as of this moment. I hear people coming.

Chapter Nine

Having a lawyer on his side was a new experience for Gil, and, it turned out, rather a pleasing one.

Vikram stood over him as the law arrived, very like a guard dog if dogs used long words and ice-edged Oxford accents instead of teeth. Even better, the Met's Inspector Ellis proved to be a lot more interested in bagging the Clare Court murderer than in asking too many questions about how and why Gil had been involved, especially when Vikram made it clear that his cooperation came with a lot of strings attached.

Not that much was needed, since Oswald admitted everything as soon as asked. It was a simple enough story. He had sold Matthew Lawes the first set of images with Errol and Sunil; Matthew had commissioned the second set, offering forty guineas for the work. Oswald had duly taken the pictures, paying the boys ten shillings each, but had not wanted to leave the matter there with such a delightfully liberal client. He'd called Errol back on the fatal Saturday to discuss further ideas for pictures. Unfortunately, he'd left Matthew's letter on a table, and Errol had seen it.

The rest was grimly inevitable. An outraged Errol demanded a larger fee for services rendered and to come; Oswald declined; Errol threatened to report him to the police for indecent images. There was an argument, and Oswald struck him, knocking him to the floor where he hit his head and died.

That last part was evident horseshit, but it hardly mattered: the police would have a doctor who could tell if Errol's wounds had been inflicted by a floor or a mallet. Either way, Oswald had dumped the body in Clare Court and then, so far as Gil could tell, gone on about his daily business while his mind squirrelled into ever smaller and tighter circles.

And that was that. Gil wouldn't even have to appear in court: there would be no need to prosecute Oswald for assault with a murder charge on the table.

"Will he hang?" Gil asked, once they were settled back in Holywell Street some hours later. His head had cleared somewhat in the interim. He had, apparently, nothing broken, and only what the doctor had called a mild concussion. It didn't feel mild. But Vikram had fussed around him since he'd got him back home, cleaning him up, lighting a fire and bringing him hot, sweet tea, and even Satan had padded silently out of the shadows to take a leap onto his lap. Gil might feel sick as a dog, but he also felt absurdly cared for, and ridiculously domestic.

"I should think so," Vikram said. "I don't see any reason to believe he wasn't in his right mind when he killed Errol. Why the devil couldn't he just pay the boys fairly in the first place?"

"Beats me. Did he say anything about Sunil?"

"Nothing useful, I fear. Errol introduced him as John Brown; Oswald had no means of contacting him. He insists he hasn't seen him since the session, and I believe him. We're back to square one there, I fear."

"Damn."

"Indeed. How are you feeling?"

"Rotten. Teach me to turn my back on a homicidal maniac."

"I was going to mention that."

"Shut up."

Vikram grinned. "Don't imagine I'll let you forget it."

Gil didn't, and the idea of Vikram sticking around to needle him about it was far too tempting. "I'm bloody glad you turned up when you did. Why did you come in?"

Vikram looked slightly embarrassed. "You'd been some time, and you'd said you wanted tea and I, er, I was worried you might be thirsty."

"You should tell the temperance people. Tea saves your life." Gil raised the mug he held in salute. "I had no idea you could handle yourself like that. Where did you learn to fight?"

"I work in Shad Thames," Vikram reminded him. "I took some lessons in self defence when I started, from a boxer. I've never had to put them into practice before."

"No? You looked like brawling was second nature."

"Well, it was a trying situation. He was swinging a mallet at me, and you were lying on the floor covered in blood. Good heavens, Gil, you frightened me. Don't do that again."

"It wasn't my idea to get hit on the head."

"You wouldn't have been hit on the head if I hadn't dragged you along. You wouldn't have been involved in any of this if I hadn't involved you." Vikram leaned over and gripped his hand. "I am so sorry."

"If you hadn't involved me, you wouldn't have found Oswald."

"No, I doubt I would."

"And he would have got off scot free. And maybe in a few weeks some other poor sod might have annoyed him, maybe another boy like Errol. I'll take a bump on the head for that."

"I still wish you hadn't had to." Vikram's fingers tightened.

Gil looked down at their entwined hands, both ink-stained for such different reasons. "Me too. And I wish we'd found out something about Sunil."

"I've had thoughts on that. We aren't giving up yet."

We, as they sat with their hands clasped in front of the gently crackling fire. Maybe it was the thump on the head, but Gil liked the sound of that.

Vikram stayed the night, putting him to bed before nine when the headache got worse, soothing him when he awoke in a sudden thrashing panic from a nightmare that mixed up a mallet-wielding lunatic, and a dead, reproachful Errol, and the dark shadowed gate of Pentonville. If Gil hadn't felt rough as dogs they could have spent those hours together in far more pleasurable ways, yet he didn't feel cheated by fate. He simply felt cared for, in a way that seeped through every hard accreted layer of defence and softened it as it went.

Vikram left early on Monday morning, locking the shop after him. He was back at lunchtime with a plate of stew and firm instructions to rest, and again in the evening, by which point Gil felt compelled to observe that he wasn't an invalid.

"You don't have to be. You can just take some time off."

"While you do all the work?"

"This isn't work. I'm enjoying it." Vikram gestured at the two of them sitting in chairs by the fireplace. He did so with some care, because Satan was draped lazily over his lap, which made sudden movements a risky business. "Talking to you. Having a little time together. Even your ghastly cat."

"He's not my cat."

"No, of course not. He just lives here. How long has he 'just lived here'?"

"Since I moved in," Gil admitted. "He turned up and wouldn't go."

"You named him, correct? You feed him. This is his sole or primary residence."

"Don't you lawyer at me."

"Gil, this is *your cat.* You have a home, a business, and a cat. It's more than I have achieved."

"You can have the cat," Gil said with feeling. "Take him."

"That's very generous of you but I imagine I'd lose an arm trying. And in any case..." Vikram met his eyes. "I'd rather share him. If you'd let me."

"I... Oh, mate. I'd love to share my cat with you." Gil's chest felt a bit tight. "But he's a fleabitten scrapper. He scratches if he thinks you're going to hurt him, even if you weren't. He's a bastard, and you could have any cat you wanted. An easy one. Something sleek and pretty that doesn't leave a trail of mouse parts. You deserve a better cat than this."

Vikram's big, elegant hand was running over Satan's long black fur. Gil could do with being stroked that way. "This fellow's had a hard life and it shows. That's not his fault. And I'd rather have my own particular fleabitten scrapper—as long as he sits on my lap now and then—than any other cat in the whole damned world."

Gil couldn't have looked away if he'd wanted to. Vikram's eyes were locked on his. "Then you're an idiot. But if this is the cat you want—"

"I've never wanted another. It's meant everything to find you, Gil. It was appalling not to know where you were, what had happened. I have missed you all my life."

Gil's chest felt a bit tight, somehow. "I'm sorry. I should have come looking for you."

"Yes, you should. And the least you can do is not leave me again. I realise that I'm an awkward, self-righteous, dogmatic nuisance, and that you have an entire life about which I know nothing, but will you *please* not abandon me? The world has been so much less enjoyable without you."

Gil's mouth was rather dry. "I'm not going anywhere. Ah, hell, Vik, listen, I need to tell you this." He really didn't want to say it. He'd spent his adult life armouring the vulnerable spots, making sure people couldn't tell where it hurt. It felt unnatural to expose himself, but Vikram needed to know. He had to force the words out, all the same. "The reason I didn't ever get in touch—well, I was afraid you'd look at me and decide you didn't want to know."

"I wouldn't—"

"No, listen. I stood my father leaving me to starve. I stood everything I did to survive. But I couldn't have stood you turning your back on me. I was too scared to try." The truth was bitter on his tongue. "Better to be where I was than to risk finding that out. I didn't stay away because you didn't matter. It was because you mattered too much. I'd lost a lot of dreams, or hopes. Memories, even—of Pa, of you, of everything before Matthew ripped my life apart. I couldn't lose any more. And I wish I'd done it differently, but I was so afraid. Can you understand that?"

"Of course I can. Of course I do, because I was afraid too." Vikram's voice sounded as raw as Gil's throat felt. "Gil, I decided you were dead. I had an enquiry agent looking for you for a month, to no effect, and then I gave up because it was more bearable to believe you were gone for good than not to know. The *not knowing* coloured everything and I couldn't tolerate it any more, but I wish I'd had the courage to keep looking more than I can say. You deserved better of me. I'm sorry."

Gil exhaled. He wasn't sure he felt better for them both getting that out, but he had a feeling he might, one day. "But you're here now. *We're* here now. And if you really want–uh, the cat, he's all yours. He might even have been waiting for you to come along, in his own stupid sort of way."

Vikram started a movement up, and froze as Satan shifted a meaningful paw. "How do I come over to you without being castrated?"

"Don't risk it." Gil got up, carefully, so his brain didn't bounce off the inside of his skull, and moved to the other chair where Vikram sat. Lowered his head so their lips met, a brush of a touch. Felt Vikram's mouth move as though he was going to say something, and pressed down harder because he'd said enough. Because all Gil needed was him and Vik kissing by the fire, tongues and lips and occasional inhalations as one or the other remembered to breathe; no more touching than that, and a pair of tangled hands. And there they were: Vik where he should have been all along; Gil letting himself believe that he wasn't going away; the both of them together.

It was even better when the cat buggered off.

Two days later, the headache finally passed. Gil still had a cracker of a bruise on his shoulder and a dark purple swelling on the side of his face, but the absence of a nagging throb in his skull felt like springtime, and he was whistling as he contemplated his shop. He'd been shut for two days and he wasn't sure he felt like opening now. Life was too good; he didn't want unkind Fate to even up the score.

Well, he'd open, and if anyone he didn't know came in hinting they wanted books unfit to print, or prints unfit to see, he'd offer them Dickens and look blank. The Society for the Suppression of Vice would get no joy from him today, and nor would anyone else. Unless they liked Dickens, of course. There was no accounting for taste.

He couldn't help but notice that, what with him being preoccupied in the last few days, his place had become a dirty bookshop in every sense, including something disembowelled under his desk, courtesy of Satan. The prospect of giving it a good clean wasn't hugely inviting, and he definitely wasn't going to start that now, but it might need to be done soon. Gil had spent a lot of the past days' enforced inactivity in thinking. He might take today to turn his thoughts into a plan.

By four that afternoon he'd done a lot of calculating, and taken a walk round to Wych Street for a bit of bargaining, and he'd decided he deserved a rest. That meant settling down behind the counter with *Jonathan*. He'd wolfed down a good half of it before Vikram had come back into his life, leaving the story with the handsome hero in chains, at the mercy of the evil guardian and his hunchbacked henchman, making protests that weren't fooling anyone. Gil had an inkling, or maybe just a hope, that the turncoat tutor who'd bedded and betrayed Jonathan might come to the rescue in the end. He was looking forward to finding out.

He sat down with a mug of tea and the precious book, and was so absorbed in the hero's pains, pleasures, and plot that he barely registered a dark shape striding meaningfully through the murk outside the window. The door flew open with a wild jangle, and Gil almost jumped out of his skin.

"Bloody hell, Vik!" he protested. "I thought you were the peelers!"

Vikram strode over, all but crackling with energy. He looked like he was about to explode, but in a good way, like a child at Christmas, and Gil couldn't help grinning in response. "What's up with you?"

"Gil," Vikram began, and then, "Back room. Now."

Startled but laughing, Gil let himself be backed into the storeroom, where Vik grabbed his face with both hands, slightly too hard for the bruising, and kissed him with some force. Gil went with it, relishing Vikram's urgent need as his own built, relishing even more that Vikram was applying his tendency to single-mindedness where it would do the most good. They ended up with Gil bumping into the table, causing the cat sleeping on his half-finished manuscript to give a yowl of protest. Vik pressed up against him, hips grinding hard together, and Gil grabbed his arse, feeling the muscle tense pleasurably under his fingers.

"Not sure what this is about," he said, muffled, "but I like it."

"It's about–" Vikram pulled back a little so Gil could see his smile. "Great Scott, I have spent all day wanting to come here and tell you but I had to go to Shad Thames first and then when I got here you distracted me."

"What? I did not."

"Yes, you did, you smiled. We found him, Gil. We *found* him. He's alive."

"He– *Sunil?*"

"Yes!" There was pure joy on Vikram's face, a slight sheen to his eyes, and all for the fate of some boy that anyone else–Gil himself—would have written off as not worth worrying about. "I had to tell his parents first. His sister's screams are still ringing in my ears. Honestly, the relief, I can't tell you."

Gil was grinning too, he realised, so widely it hurt his face. "Alive. That's marvellous. Sodding marvellous. Where the hell was he?"

Vikram coughed. "In gaol. He was arrested for disorderly conduct that Saturday night, and got twenty-eight days. He'll be out at the end of the week."

"Oh, for God's sake. Did you not say your man had looked into that?"

"For Sunil Gupta. It dawned on me that he might be using his John Brown alias, so I gave my investigator that name on Monday and he came back this morning. I went to see him. It's him."

Gil settled back against the table. "Well, now. How is he?"

"Subdued, afraid, and unhappy, but not harmed. Mostly concerned that his parents will be angry, as well he might be. I told him I would intervene to smooth matters over if he agreed to accept assistance in finding alternative employment once he's released."

Gil lifted a brow. "Taking a bit on yourself there, aren't you?"

"Perhaps," Vikram admitted. "But I feel I owe him a great deal. If I hadn't looked for him, I wouldn't have found you."

Gil didn't entirely agree that constituted an obligation, since Sunil hadn't exactly got himself arrested as a philanthropic act, but he wasn't going to argue, not with Vik this close and the satisfaction rolling off him. He probably didn't get enough victories, and if the boy was alive that was a hell of a thing. "What are you going to do with him?"

"I have no idea," Vikram said frankly. "I didn't think that far ahead. I need to speak to him further, find out his capabilities and interests. I know he can read, but that's all. I am aware I rather rushed in."

"You do that. Mph. Well."

Vikram gave him a hopeful look. "Do you have an idea?"

He sort of had one. Gil had never taken on help in the shop before. It had felt like a risk he didn't want to run and a responsibility he didn't want to have. He was no William Dugdale to put his faith in some bright, hungry, scrappy boy and trust him to be loyal.

But maybe a man with a home and a cat and a—well, call it a someone who was willing to put up with the cat—might hire a lad to sweep the floor, and if that lad was bright and personable and could learn how to sell something that wasn't himself, that might even work.

"I could use him in here for a bit," he suggested. "He already knows what's what so he'll keep his mouth shut. Unless you wouldn't want him involved, of course, but—"

Vikram grimaced. "I did rather have in mind getting him away from this trade."

"That's going to be up to him," Gil pointed out. "It's easy to say *do something else,* but he's been bringing in good money with no heavy lifting for a while. A month in chokey won't have been fun, but nor is scrimping and saving and sweating for every penny when you know you can get a couple of days' meals for your family for an hour's effort."

"Granted, but—"

"And I'm selling up."

Vikram stilled. "I beg your pardon?"

"Selling up. I don't want to end up like Dugdale either, in and out of gaol all my life. The hell with that, now Matthew's dead."

Vikram frowned. "What difference does that make? Are you feeling confused again?"

"I'm not confused, though I might be an idiot. Matthew pushed me into the gutter, and I stayed in it because it felt like a sod-you to him, and all the rest of them who agreed that's where I belonged in the first place. But if he ever cared about that, and I doubt he did, he's dead now. And to be honest, if I had been paying attention instead of trying to find a way to blame him for Sunil, I might not have got hit on the head at all. Oswald fed me a line about Matthew's involvement to distract me, and it worked, because I'm still letting that arsehole get to me from beyond the grave. I need to scrape him off my shoes. I should have done that a long time ago."

"I do *wish* he was still alive," Vikram said, with a combination of wistful longing and malevolent intent that made Gil want to kiss him. "But I interrupted you."

"I'm used to it. Where was I?"

"Selling up. Really?"

Gil nodded. "I don't enjoy getting the wind up every time you throw a door open like you want to take it off its hinges. I think it's time to get out of this game, open the kind of bookshop that won't get me arrested. So I could use someone to help me get the stock dealt with, and maybe he might want to stick around and learn the trade. And even if he doesn't, I might have something to say that he'd listen to."

Vikram nodded slowly. "I suppose he might find it easier to speak frankly to you than to me."

Gil contemplated Vikram's manicured nails and tailored suit. "Could be, lawyer."

"Would you do that?"

"I'll give him a few days' work here, and I'll have a chat with him while I'm about it. But nobody's going to save him if he doesn't feel there's something to be saved from. You hold a hand out, and let him decide whether to take it. Trying to force him won't work."

"I think I understand that better than I used to," Vikram said. "Though it seems to me it would be you holding the hand out. Ah, since I have rather foisted this on you, may I be responsible—"

"Matthew's paying," Gil said over him. "I've got a bloke from Wych Street coming tomorrow to take all the photographs off my hands—or most of them, I've set aside the ones with Sunil and poor bloody Errol for burning. It's a bargain for him, but it's still more than enough to cover a decent wage for as long as I need."

"If you're sure. Won't moving and setting up again be expensive?"

"I've got my inheritance and my savings, and Matthew's collection was worth a fair bit. I'm splitting the proceeds with Percy but it'll still be a tidy sum." That was not including *Jonathan*. He rather thought he'd keep that for himself. "I'll do nicely. You have no idea how respectable I'm going to be."

The smile in Vikram's eyes was everything. "I would love you to be respectable in public. Ah, in private, though...?"

"Oh, in private, sod respectability for a game of soldiers. Come here."

He had his arse propped against the edge of the table still. He hopped up to sit on it properly as Vikram walked in between his legs like he was born to be there, and wrapped his thighs around Vik's hips. Vikram leaned down for a kiss, lips meeting Gil's with a care that rapidly turned to open-mouthed urgency, and Gil grabbed his shoulders and pulled him close, getting a hand into that thick hair, feeling Vik's hand in his own curls. Gripping one another, tangled up in each other like they always had been, still were, and not looking to change.

And maybe this was just the shabby back room of a dirty Holywell Street bookshop, but he had Vikram quivering with pleasure in his arms, the smell of books and ink and beautiful lawyer in his nose, some of those hopes and dreams he'd abandoned rising up again as if they'd never really gone away, and that was pretty much all Gil could have asked from life, right here.

The cat would probably come with him when he moved, but you couldn't have everything.

The End

This book was named by Sherene Khaw in my Facebook group, KJ Charles Chat. Thanks to all the Chatters for making this fun.

With special thanks to Talia Hibbert and Elena Meyer-Bothling, to Veronica Vega for knowing the words I actually meant as opposed to the ones I typed, and to Lennan Adams for the gorgeous cover.

A Charm of Magpies world

The Magpie Lord
A Case of Possession
Flight of Magpies
Jackdaw
A Queer Trade
Rag and Bone

Society of Gentlemen series

The Ruin of Gabriel Ashleigh
A Fashionable Indulgence
A Seditious Affair
A Gentleman's Position

Sins of the Cities series

An Unseen Attraction
An Unnatural Vice
An Unsuitable Heir

Standalone books

Think of England
The Secret Casebook of Simon Feximal
Wanted, a Gentleman
The Price of Meat
The Henchmen of Zenda
Spectred Isle
Band Sinister

Praise for KJ Charles

"A romp of a novella. … a perfectly compact romance that shows a couple can be cranky and still head-over-heels for each other."

—Romantic Times on *Wanted, a Gentleman*, Top Pick and Seal of Excellence

"This novel combines romance with paranormal fear and humour perfectly ... a lovely mix of Nietzsche, Poe, and pure K.J. Charles."

—All About Romance on *The Secret Casebook of Simon Feximal*

"KJ Charles has long been one of my favorite authors, and this book doesn't disappoint. *A Seditious Affair* is a beautiful love story interwoven with the realism of the political unrest of the time—another winner from KJ Charles!"

—USA Today bestselling author Carole Mortimer

"The realities of class, societal mores and politics heighten the tension in this emotional, deeply romantic look at the remarkable lengths we will go for love."

—Washington Post on *A Gentleman's Position*

"A plot that's unabashed pulp, made poignant by its effects on the two bruised souls at its center."

—Publishers' Weekly on *An Unseen Attraction*, starred review

"Watching two guarded men trade arch Lost Generation banter while edging closer and closer to romance is deeply satisfying; the book's wry, anguished, darkly witty prose will make it perfect for the coming rains of autumn."

—Seattle Review of Books on *Spectred Isle*

"*The Magpie Lord* is a witty, action-packed sexy-as-hell fantasy romance. Tattoo a magpie on my heart and keep the Stephen and Crane stories coming. I'm in lust!"

—Tiffany Reisz, international bestselling and award-winning author of The Original Sinners series

"The always-reliable K.J. Charles outdoes herself with *The Henchmen of Zenda* ... there is swashbuckling, double and triple crossing, intrigue, a moat, a castle, smart women, and hot sex. What's not to like?"

—Smart Bitches, Trashy Books on *The Henchmen of Zenda*

About the Author

KJ Charles is a RITA®-nominated romance writer and editor. She lives in London with her husband, two kids, a garden with quite enough prickly things, and a cat with murder management issues.

Find her at kjcharleswriter.com for book info, blogging, and sign-up for her infrequent newsletter with book news and freebies. KJ is all too often on Twitter @kj_charles, and has a lively Facebook group, KJ Charles Chat, for conversation, sneak peeks and group exclusives.

Lightning Source UK Ltd.
Milton Keynes UK
UKHW022017260922
409492UK00012B/198